# EVERYTHING WENT HAYW

The German guards were rudely awakened from their sleep by the demolition thunder of the explosive charges that had been planted all over Stalag 20.

Fully briefed, the POWs jumped the Wehrmacht guards stationed in each barracks building. Arming themselves with the captured guns and grenades and makeshift weapons of their own devising, they bolted outside and stormed the prison compound.

By then the uniformed soldiers were trooping out of their barracks, letting loose a barrage of small-arms fire, and the machine-gunners in the crow's nests on the camp perimeter trained their heavy caliber chatterguns on the prisoners who overran the base.

Glowing dots and dashes stitched downward through the blackness of the night, and scores of prisoners were cut down in midstride. But in no time flat the human wave of men was surging in a bloodstained tide through the gaping rupture torn in Stalag 20's main gate.

Overwhelmed by the sheer force of numbers, the Germans brought up two armored cars and a Panzer Mark IV tank. The Panzer was armed with a 105 mm howitzer cannon, and with the savage tolling of man-made thunder, it started hurling deadly high explosive shells into the camp.

# OKLAHOMA

## SOLDIERS OF WAR

## COMPANY OF HEROES
### William Reed

**A GOLD EAGLE BOOK FROM**
# WORLDWIDE.

TORONTO · NEW YORK · LONDON · PARIS
AMSTERDAM · STOCKHOLM · HAMBURG
ATHENS · MILAN · TOKYO · SYDNEY

Mobilized for active duty in 1940, the 45th Infantry Division was baptized in blood during the death struggle to free Europe. The Thunderbirds of the Oklahoma National Guard slogged through the muddiest, bloodiest miles of World War II. Oklahoma's National Guard was ready to answer the call, just as it is today. This book is dedicated to the Guard's brave soldiers, wherever they may serve.

*This is a work of fiction and, except in the case of major historical figures and events, makes no attempt whatsoever to portray actual persons and situations or to document actual occurrences. This is purely and completely a work of the imagination.*

First edition July 1991

ISBN 0-373-63402-1

Special thanks and acknowledgment to
David Alexander for his contribution to this work.

COMPANY OF HEROES

# BOOK ONE:
# The Calm Before the Storm

Naples, Italy
July to August, 1944

**1**

*Naples*

Private First Class Frankie "Mutt" Babcock didn't know how he came to be making whoopee with both Dorothy Lamour and Rita Hayworth at the same time, and he didn't much care. The only thing he knew was that it was even more fun than getting the best of the Germans, his favorite pastime.

"Gee, you dames is sure swell," Mutt cried out as he cavorted with his two favorite film starlets in a gigantic swimming pool. "In fact, you dames is the berries."

Suddenly the round, firm bosoms of the swell jane that Mutt had been clutching in his hot hands changed into the horns of a ferocious fire-snorting bull. Mutt gave out a horrified scream and tried to run. But giant plants sprouted up out of the ground and wrapped sticky tentacles around his legs, pinning him fast.

Next thing Mutt knew, he was at the center of a bullring. In his hands was a red cape, and he was dressed in a matador's uniform. The nightmarish bull charged him again, its head low, the horns ready to gore his stomach. But just before it made contact, the bull turned into an SS stormtrooper charging him with bayonet fixed to the barrel of his Gewehr assault rifle. Shouting *"Heil Hitler,"* the trooper stabbed Mutt right through the heart.

Mutt awoke with half his body on the floor and the other half on the bed from which he'd fallen with a loud thump. He could smell the hot wind coming off the streets of Naples and could hear the sounds of footsteps, shouts and the wheels of ox-drawn carts trundling through the cobblestoned alley running directly below the window.

Two men were having an argument in Neapolitan somewhere outside. Mutt's mother was Italian and used to speak it at home all the time, but he couldn't understand a word of the local dialect. They spoke it here in Naples and no place else.

A moment later the memory of where he really was started coming back with all the force of a sledgehammer blow. Mutt didn't want to be reminded how he had gotten to be in the room, because something told him that he wouldn't like it. He temporarily pushed the memory aside and sprang to his feet.

He had to answer the call of nature in a bad way. Mutt staggered out into the hall toward the bathroom, but the toilet was overflowing. So he sidled over to the little toilet to the right, the one they called a bidet. What the fuck is a bidet anyway? he muttered to himself. Only the Italians and the French would have two kinds of pissers in their bathrooms.

His head splitting, Mutt staggered toward the washbasin in the corner. Sticking his head inside the basin of the sink and turning on the tap, he let the cold water gush down the back of his neck.

"Mary, Joseph and all the saints," he groaned as he felt the top of his head. "What have I gotten myself into now?"

Staggering over to the dresser facing the bed, Mutt braced himself with both arms against the top and stared into the dresser's mirror. Though he had half expected what he next saw, the shock was not diminished in the least.

They had shaved Mutt's head completely, but they had not done too damned neat a job. Tufts of fuzz sprouted here and there on the otherwise cueball-clean dome.

The worst was yet to come, though. Mutt looked down and suddenly remembered the tattooist. The tattooist had come from Palermo, he recalled. He had claimed he did very good work and immediately proceeded to demonstrate to the drunken American.

Mutt now took stock of the tattooist's handiwork. On his right arm was a big red heart, pierced by an arrow from one end to the other. Beneath the heart was inscribed the name Isabella. Above his right nipple was the word Heaven and above the left, the word Hell.

But the tattooist from Palermo had saved his pièce de résistance for last, Mutt now recalled—and fully appreciated just how anesthetized he must have been by the alcohol. He had tattooed Mutt's virile member in a manner resembling the poles that stood in front of barber shops back home in Oklahoma City. His manly stave was now corkscrewed with red-and-white stripes. The only thing missing was the cigar-store Indian.

Christ, what a disaster, Mutt thought. First he got drafted into the Army. Then Betty Grable married Harry James and broke his heart. Now this happened. A German bullet right through the ticker would have been a pleasure compared to the kind of trouble Mutt now was in.

With a king-size headache hammering at him, Mutt searched the room for his clothes, but knew from the first that the Neapolitan prostitutes and their grease-ball pimp had stolen everything. Actually they hadn't, Mutt soon realized. They had left him a single article of clothing. A baggy woman's dress decorated with a floral pattern.

Mutt threw it on and stole from the house into the street, grateful that it was still early in the morning and few pedestrians were about. In any case, those few early risers among the citizenry of Naples cared little about an American GI who furtively groped his way along the time-stained building walls attired in such a manner. They had seen many strange goings-on since the Americans had landed on their ancient shores.

At first, sights such as this had prompted comments and derisive gestures poking fun at the insanity of the Americans, but the locals now barely lifted an eyebrow. The Neapolitans were a people accustomed to witnessing many strange sights in their long and complicated history. The American in the dress was just another one of these.

"PSSST! HEY, YOU GUYS!"

Privates Buddy Kelso and Haystacks Jones were taking a morning ramble along the quaintly cobbled streets of Naples, enhancing the salutary effects of fresh sea air and the wholesome exercise of walking with liberal swigs from a jug of dark red wine they had promoted from the shop of a local merchant.

Kelso and Haystacks were Thunderbirds themselves, just like Mutt. They were attached to the forty-fifth Infantry Division's 179th Regiment of the Oklahoma National Guard. The patches on the right sleeves of their no-longer-fresh "A" uniforms bore the divisional insignia of the ancient Amerindian thunderbird. Originally the insignia had been a swastika. Before Hitler had come along, that is.

But there was an even closer connection. Mutt, Kelso and Haystacks were all attached to Dog Company. The company had acquired its name because on an inspection tour their commander, Captain "Smilin' Mike" Calhoun, had remarked that Company D "was the dogginest lookin' bunch of flea-scratchin' dog-faces in the whole doggone Army." He also said that he'd be dog-damned if he called Company D anything but "Dog Company" from there on in. Not unpredictably the name had stuck.

*"Hey, you guys! Psst! Over here!"*

In their pleasantly winy haze, Kelso and Haystacks did double takes as they squinted toward the voice issuing from the shadows of the urine-reeking alley they had just passed.

"Who the fuck's squawkin'?" asked Kelso, craning his neck in an attempt to cut through the murk but succeeding only in sighting a stray alley cat. "If that's Bee-Lips Willie from Quartermaster Corps, we don't owe you a fuckin' dime."

"Yeah, you mug, we're paid up, see!" shouted the drunken Haystacks, brandishing his fist and yawing back and forth like a sapling in the wind.

"It ain't Bee-Lips Willie. It's your buddy Mutt," the voice from the shadows of the alley cried again. "I'm in a real bad jam."

"Holy fucking cow, Mutt, how come you to be attired in such an unseemly manner?" Kelso asked as he and Haystacks stepped into the mouth of the alley and saw Mutt in his full glory. "Not that it don't become you," he added with a smirk when Mutt stepped into view.

"You think it becomes him, Haystacks?"

"Like it was made for him," Haystacks returned deadpan. "I ain't kidding. It is unseemly but it is still becoming."

The doughfoots hadn't seen their buddy Mutt since well before the beginning of their platoon's thirty-six-hour leave. They had been wondering what the hell had happened to him, figuring he'd been either bumped off by the locals or arrested by the MPs. Either way, they figured he might not be joining them for the invasion of France that every dogface knew was coming.

"It's a long story," Mutt told them. "But I'm in a real pickle. You guys gotta help me promote a uniform, or they'll stick my ass in the guardhouse for the duration and throw away the key."

Mutt quickly explained how he had been taken in by a trio of good-looking Neapolitan dames who had kept him drunk on grappa for the past couple of days. During that time they had stolen his uniform and everything he had on him. For some unexplainable reason they had also tattooed his entire body.

"No sweat, Chet," Kelso and Haystacks put in. "Just leave everything to us."

A couple of minutes later the cobbled Neapolitan streets echoed with the cadence of smartly stepping army boots. Kelso and Haystacks nodded to each other.

The perfect victim came sauntering down the street. It was one of the rear-guard jockeys, a paper-pusher if they'd ever seen one. The officer was practically measured for a sucker punch. His lieutenant's bars practically cried out for a sock in the choppers.

With his uniform pressed so sharply that the creases in his pants could slit your throat, his cap canted at the precise angle described in the GI training manual, his campaign boots spit-polish bright, he purposefully walked along, whistling "Lili Marlene." He was a chump made in heaven.

As the officer came abreast of the narrow alleyway, he was suddenly confronted by Kelso, who wore a broad grin on his lean-jowled face.

"Uh, 'scuze me, mack," Kelso drawled at the officer, keeping his head low to hide his face as much as possible. "If it's nine o'clock in Casablanca, what time is it in Pittsburgh?"

"Sure thing," replied the rear-guard officer, who figured he hadn't heard the soldier correctly and by pure reflex action raised his watch hand to his face in order to tell the time. Before he knew what hit him, Haystacks threw a gunnysack they had picked up in the street over his head.

Moving fast, Mutt and Kelso launched a series of hard lefts and rights to the victim's breadbasket. A few moments later the officer was sprawled in the alley, stripped to his skivvies and knocked out cold.

"Thanks, boys. I won't forget what you done," Mutt said with a throb of genuine emotion in his voice. Tipping a swallow of vino into his mouth, he strolled down Naples's cobbled streets with Kelso and Haystacks, the words to a new Kay Kyser tune on his lips.

**2**

General Alexander Patch, commander of the U.S. Seventh Army, stood before a large illuminated map on the wall of the briefing room. Red circles and black arrows indicated strike zones and attack vectors across a landscape torn and gutted by the ravages of total war.

The vast salon was decorated in the grand style of European royalty. Its ceiling was ornamented with lozenge-shaped lunettes filled with colorful frescoes by the greatest painters of Europe. The great meeting hall was located in a villa overlooking the Tyrrhenian Sea at the top of one of the city's highest hills and positioned for its breathtaking view.

From the windows of the villa a spectator could gaze across the Tyrrhenian and see the eastern coastline of the island of Sardinia. Beyond this ancient island populated by a secretive and isolated people, there lay Corsica and beyond that, the Gulf of Lions. It was there in the gulf that the Oklahomans of the Forty-fifth Infantry Division would soon be deployed, sent out to fight, bleed and die.

The Allied assaults on Utah, Omaha, Gold, Juno and Sword—the beaches of Normandy—had been a success the previous June. Hitler and his minions had been caught napping. Literally so, for the story went that Panzer tanks critical to German defenses were not deployed when none had the courage to awaken the slumbering Führer.

The Allies had landed men and matériel in force from their vast armada lying offshore. As expected, the invasion force was challenged by ferocious German firepower from well-positioned troops dug in behind the line of concrete bunkers, slit trenches and underground bunkers that comprised fortifications known as the German's Atlantic Wall. In the end, U.S., British and Canadian forces had secured the beachheads and were now advancing at a slow but respectable pace.

That was in June. Now, in August, the game plan called for a second invasion of France, this time from its southern coast. Within a matter of hours, the formations under Patch's command would be embarking on their own assault. This invasion was to be aimed at the enemy's second flank.

The assault to be staged on the southern coast of Nazi-occupied France differed from the Normandy invasion in two principal respects. First, the Germans were no longer committed to a strategy of digging in and weathering any Allied assault. Retreat was no longer a word to be spoken in hushed tones at the Oberkommando Der Wehrmacht, or German High Command. Here, the enemy could not commit the firepower, and here they also lacked the coastal defenses of the Atlantic Wall.

Second, this follow-up assault on France would be staged just after the break of dawn. The enemy had become conditioned to expect Allied landings in the predawn hours, and was ready for the same timing. A very intricate deception campaign by the Allies would insure that the Germans miscalculated. With a little luck, Patch's troops could catch the Germans with their pants down.

"Gentlemen," Patch said to the assemblage he faced, a gathering of officers under his command. "We have received orders from Ike. Unless you are informed otherwise within the next few hours, the attack is to commence as scheduled."

Patch held his pointing stick and indicated a semicircular stretch of coastline toward which three arrows were aimed. The legend beneath the first arrow identified the U.S. Sixth Corps under the command of Lieutenant General Lucian Truscott.

"Six Corps under Truscott is to sweep in from the northwest. They will comprise the first wave." The general then used the pointer to indicate yet another cutting edge of the Allied spearhead.

"Here the Free French Forces will comprise a fast-striking salient of the three-pronged assault."

Next Patch located his own soldiers. The Forty-fifth Infantry would make up the sharp central tine of the Allied trident aimed at the heart of the coastal region of the south of France.

"That's us right there, gentlemen," he said, pointing at the central spearhead of the Allied invasion force. "We will comprise the backbone of the invasion force. We're going in near Sainte-Maxime. It's a major coastal center. The Germans have it lightly garrisoned. But they have deployed their heavy guns inland, as well as Panzer tanks and perhaps rocket launchers. It won't be a cakewalk. Any questions?"

"General, what about German infantry?" one of Patch's commanding officers asked. "The boys at

Normandy got beat up pretty badly by entrenched Nazi troops.''

"Intelligence reports indicate that the steam has been taken out of the German military machine here in the south," Patch returned unhesitatingly. "In all likelihood the German combat strategy will be to engage our forces in an attempt to pin them down and allow their own forces to retreat to their rear. That, we are confident, is their primary objective."

"What about tanks, sir?" another officer asked.

"General Blaskowitz of the German Army Group G is known to have Panzer reserves stationed here, at Aix-en-Provence," Patch said, again picking up his pointer. "How many, and how quickly they will be able to deploy their armor, is still an unknown quantity."

"At Normandy the Germans had everything booby-trapped," another officer put in, referring to the network of antipersonnel mines and explosive mantraps that Field Marshal Rommel had ordered placed in the swampland and fields directly behind the beachheads. "I'm concerned about the same contingency here in the south. What have we got to look at here, sir?"

"From all accounts, the Germans have not had the time, resources or the manpower to put out the same kind of welcoming mat for us this time around," the general responded.

"Another factor that makes the assault on the south less likely to result in unsustainable losses is that the French underground here has been harassing the Germans every step of the way, working in conjunction with the OSS. The enemy is more intent on withdrawing with his forces intact than in fighting to stay,'' he concluded. ''They know that they have absolutely no hope of achieving this objective.''

General Patch picked up his pointer and turned to face the map. He outlined the thrust of the Allied forces up through the spine of the mountains of southern France once the beachhead had finally been secured.

After that the Allied armies would sweep up through the central portion of France in a broad salient until they linked up with Allied forces sweeping down from the north.

''There it is, men,'' the general concluded, turning to face his staff again. ''Operation Dragoon. Good luck and God bless you.''

As the officers filed out of the briefing room, General Patch turned to stare out the window across the Tyrrhenian and up the western coastline of Italy. Somewhere out there, beyond the expanse of glittering ocean, the coast of southern France was waiting. And on it, a giant specter waited, too. He was the Pale Horseman, and his name was Death.

## 3

Sergeant Joe Minnevitch sat with a bunch of cards clutched in his big hands and the dead stump of a five-cent Philly cigar jutting out of the corner of his mouth, just to one side of the puckered scar running down the other.

He wore his hair shaved right down to the scalp with only a crest like a Mohawk brave's at the top. This was inspired by the paratroopers at Normandy. The haircut and his steel gray eyes made Minnevitch one fearsome-looking son of a bitch.

Minnevitch was the son of Ruthenian immigrants from the Russian-Romanian border who had made landfall at Ellis Island in New York City and kept on traveling westward. They had stopped their traveling when they hit the Great Plains of Oklahoma. There they decided to settle, opening up a hardware store in Tulsa.

The store eventually became a chain of stores that netted them a small fortune each year. Although his family's money and connections could have kept Minnevitch out of the Army altogether, he had enlisted anyway, despite his father's objections. Minnevitch wanted to serve his country and punish by fire and steel those who dared oppose the principles of democracy, individualism and free enterprise—the principles that made his country great.

Originally mustered in as a buck private, Minnevitch had worked his way up through the ranks by way of a series of field promotions for bravery under fire. Getting wounded in the leg at Salerno had rated him corporal's stripes and a Purple Heart.

Mortar shrapnel at Anzio had added a third chevron to his rank and a Silver Star, which he vowed to wear only after demobilization, if the day ever came, or if he lived that long—whichever came first. It had also earned him another Purple Heart.

Minnevitch was a combat veteran and then some, and he had the wounds all over to prove it.

He and the boys were playing knock poker in an old brick warehouse located near the Naples docks. To one side of Minnevitch sat Eddie Dunn and Bobby Fontana, two dogfaces from his outfit, Dog Company's First Platoon. Dunn was a private first class and Fontana a buck private.

Another one of the dogfaces in the game, Jake Gridley, was attached to the Quartermaster Corps. Gridley was amplifying his meager combat pay by selling Neapolitan plaster saints to the Army, only the Army didn't know about it and, due to Gridley's clever accounting methods, thought they were buying field blankets. The warehouse was where the people he was doing business with stashed the saints.

Though he outranked every man at the card table, pulling rank with this bunch wouldn't do Minnevitch a lick of good. When it came to knock poker, they were all equals. The only thing that counted here and now was the hand that he'd been dealt, and it wasn't a damned good one.

*"Assholes and elbows, you chicken-scratchin' meatballs. This here's a raid!"*

Suddenly MPs were swarming over the place, having smashed down the door and stormed the warehouse, swinging their truncheons with a vengeance. "From now on, you lame-brained galoots are gonna be gettin' your mail care of the guardhouse. In case you mugs don't know it, there's strict orders against gambling in this town. You're also fraternizing with the locals. *Now, up against the wall.*"

Some members of the force of military policemen waded into the game while other MPs stationed themselves at the exits, truncheons in their hands and scowls on their chunky faces. The dogfaces sitting around the poker table flung down their cards faster than you can say "hit the dirt."

None of them had any problems with getting killed for the red, white and blue. But sitting out the war behind bars was another matter entirely.

Minnevitch was out of his seat in practically a second flat. The MP who had come after him put a beefy mitt on his shoulder. The guy was a regular hulk, and one mean son of a bitch just from the looks of him, with a bull neck and little red eyes and a throat dewlapped like a Thanksgiving turkey. He thought he had the sergeant's number.

But Minnevitch lashed out with a stiff-armed elbow smash that pushed the MP's hand away. The MP was stunned, and he brought up his billy club, swinging straight for Minnevitch's noggin.

Minnevitch ducked under the powerful swing that would have pulverized his skull, and delivered a series of lightning lefts, rights and uppercuts to the MP's head, chest and beer-barrel gut. Minnevitch had learned the art of pugilism on the streets and in the alleys of San Francisco.

He'd left Oklahoma to go to school in the Bay City, but instead frequented the opium dens in the Wharf District. After a while he had fallen in with gangsters and rumrunners. He had left school to become a permanent rumrunner, loving the bootlegger's life. It was only the repeal of Prohibition that had ended the outlaw's life for Minnevitch and left a hungering for action in his soul, an appetite that only the Second World War could satisfy.

The locals sitting at the table took off like river rats deserting a leaky scow, leaving only Minnevitch, Dunn, Fontana and Gridley behind to duke it out with the shit-flies. That was okay, though. With three Thunderbirds plus Gridley up against a dozen-odd club-swinging MPs, the fight was at least a fair one.

Fontana cursed in Sicilian and whipped out a long, sharp knife and picked his man. He'd been skinning rabbits at fifty paces until he'd gotten shipped overseas. Since then, it had been the Nazis who'd been getting their hides removed through Fontana's bladesmanship.

As Fontana shot off a string of insults against several generations of the MP's family, he unleashed two quick knife throws in succession that pinned the MP against the wall by the sleeve of his shirt. A solid kick of Fontana's steel-toed combat boot to the crotch of another military cop beside him put that guy out of commission, too.

Private Dunn was using the heavy oak card table as a shield as the other MPs closed in, pinning three of them to the wall at once. Minnevitch and Gridley punched out their lights before they could squirm loose.

"Let's get out of here!" hollered Minnevitch as they vaulted over the dazed and unconscious MPs and bolted for the back door, only to find more MPs waiting outside, their eyes agleam, and smacking truncheons against their palms.

Before another punch was thrown, though, giant fishing nets came sailing down from the warehouse rooftop. The locals hadn't entirely deserted their GI Joe poker buddies after all, and as the MPs struggled in the nets like big ugly fish, the dogfaces made tracks.

"*Arrivederci!*" the locals shouted after them from the rooftop, before they too melted into the night.

CATERINA'S MOTHER buried her face in her handkerchief. She always cried at weddings. So why shouldn't she cry extra hard at the wedding of her own daughter? Especially considering the special circumstances in which it took place.

It had come as a shock when the family had found out that Caterina was carrying the American soldier's child. Her father had wanted to kill the American, but then it turned out that the American was willing to marry Caterina.

Things looked much better, especially since they'd discovered that the American, though a lowly corporal, had a great deal of money.

Caterina's mother did not understand at first how a simple farmer could be so rich, but then the American had explained how the cows on his father's farm were of a breed unique to the pastures of Oklahoma.

This breed was one that gave sugared milk, and so was in great demand.

The sugared milk of the American's cows had made the American's family extremely wealthy. This changed matters entirely. Caterina now would be the wife of a rich American.

It had probably saved the American's life. The family had been intent on giving him "the necktie." Such a necktie was the last gift one would normally receive.

As he stood at the altar with his new bride, Corporal Johnny Amboy was sweating bullets. He had no intention of being married, but what could he do? The three goons with their arms crossed were watching him like chicken hawks. Amboy knew these creeps were Mafia.

They had described in graphic detail the fate that awaited him if Amboy did not marry their deflowered sister. Amboy would be seated in a chair and a stiletto knife drawn across his throat.

The blood that poured down the front of his chest would be what the Neapolitans called "the necktie." The Neapolitans didn't give a hoot in hell about what the U.S. military authorities might say afterward. Honor demanded action, and who were the Americans to interfere with local customs, anyway?

"Do you, John Amboy take Caterina Ferro to be your lawful wedded wife?" asked the priest.

Before Amboy could respond the air filled with the choking smoke of stink bombs. Amboy felt hands grabbing his arms.

"Forget the eytie dame. You're coming with us, Amboy."

"B-but—" Amboy spluttered.

"But me no buts," one of his buddies told him. "We just got orders to ship out. You wanna come with us and kill some heinies or eat cold spaghetti the rest of your life?"

Amboy didn't even have time to wave farewell to Caterina and his unborn child. Nor were her three brothers in time to grab him, because they were out like lights, courtesy of Amboy's buddies. Whether he liked it or not, Amboy was now on his way to help make the world a safer place.

**4**

Lieutenant Hank J. Canfield swore that when he got his mitts on the eight-balls who had hit him with a cheap shot, he was going to get even. Boiling them in oil wouldn't even be good enough for those yeggs. He would have to think up something special to pay them back. Boy, would they ever be sorry.

Canfield had been walking down the street minding his own damned business when the mother-hunchin' bastards had jumped him. They had stolen his uniform and left him in a stinking alleyway with two busted ribs, a fractured jaw and a shiner as big as the October moon over an Oklahoma wheat field.

The face of the gorilla who had sucker-punched him was a face that Canfield would remember for a long time to come. That long, sallow-jowled mug and that big toothy grin that reminded him of a Halloween pumpkin's evil smile. You didn't see an ugly kisser like that every day. Not even in a rough-and-tumble town like Naples.

Canfield had a personal score to settle with that lame-brained numskull. And when he got his meat hooks on him, he'd make him give up his two buddies. That and war bonds you could take to the bank.

But Canfield had other matters on his mind right at the moment. His own unit was being absorbed into other elements of the southern France invasion force. Canfield was now being given command of a new unit.

A unit known as D-Company.

THE NAPLES DOCKS were thronged with servicemen weighted down with full combat gear. Doughfoots griped and motor vehicles groaned, their laboring engines protesting much like the GIs who drove them as they were trundled up ramps to sit idle in the holds of Liberty Ships until deployment time came.

The harbor was congested with seagoing warcraft of every shape, size and description, flying the colors of four nations. From the big Liberty Ships to corvettes to the landing barges that would storm the beachheads of the French Riviera, the water of the harbor was black with the steel leviathans that would ferry the assault waves to storm the enemy beachheads of occupied France.

Sergeant Joe Minnevitch and Dog Company's First Platoon sat around waiting to be summoned to board the Liberty Ship that was to bring them to within sight of the French coastline.

The sarge, privates Fontana, Dunn, Corporal Amboy and a couple of other Dog Company dogfaces were shooting craps, knowing that the MPs weren't about to bother them here. Dunn was making out like a bandit, throwing sixes and sevens as though the dice were on fire.

It was not due to skill or even luck. Dunn had no skill to speak of and didn't believe in luck, except maybe the bad kind. Dunn believed in Dunn, so he had marked the dice in a manner passed down through ten generations of Dunns, including his father, who had left an English penal colony to start over fresh in America.

In the general confusion of mobilization before the assault, the GIs who had escaped the raid on the warehouse poker game had gotten completely lost in the scuffle. Enemy lead might end up killing them, but mobilization had some saving graces, too. Under other circumstances, each man would have found himself facing a court-martial tribunal. Now nobody was looking too hard for them.

A couple of hundred yards from First Platoon's location, the dogfaces of Second Platoon were sitting around on their butts. Mutt, Kelso and Haystacks were cleaning their weapons. Other GIs were reading letters from home or staring out to sea, their eyes and minds looking ahead to the coming storm.

Haystacks and Kelso packed M-1s while Mutt had a Thompson submachine gun he had succeeded in drawing from the company's armor artificer, who owed him some favors. Mutt was the best man with a tommy gun in the unit. He thought it made a nice sound to the ear as it mowed down the enemy.

The doughfoots had cleaned and oiled each weapon countless times, but once more couldn't hurt, and besides, there wasn't much else to do. Kelso called his weapon "the Heinie Killer" because of the fifty Germans he'd sent to hell with it, and he had the notches on the buttstock to prove it.

The Army was again playing its game of "hurry up and wait." It worked in the usual predictable manner: the men were called up for mobilization, trucked and ferried toward the front, only to be made to sit on their backsides for hours, days or weeks until it was finally time to mobilize.

Having finished with his gun, Mutt got out a V-Mail blank. He decided to kill some time by writing another letter to his favorite screen actress, Rita Hayworth.

He began his letter, licking the point of his pencil.

Dear Rita,
I think you're a swell dame. You sure got a load of what it takes to please a man, if you get my drift. I bet that goes double for the places that don't show. I'd sure like to find out sometime. When I'm on the front lines killing heinies in France and Germany, I'll be thinking of the beautiful music you and me could make together.

Your Greatest Fan,
Franklin M. Babcock

Tinker, another Thunderbird, happened to be looking over Mutt's shoulder as he wrote his fan letter. "You writing to that Hayworth dame again?" he asked.

"You maybe got a squawk with that?" Mutt shot back, sensitive about his writing and covering the V-Mail blank with his left hand as he glared at the dogface.

"No, I ain't got no squawk, except that you should be writing to a real looker, not some Hollywood has-been." Before Mutt could sock him right in the choppers, Tinker fished around in the pockets of his field jacket and pulled out a crumpled color picture torn from a calendar.

He unfolded the paper and held it in front of Mutt's face. "Here's what I call a real dame," he said admiringly. "Betty Grable. Hubba-hubba. Ruff! Ruff! What I wouldn't give to be the spider on her bedroom wall."

Suddenly the shrill whistle signaled that Dog Company was to board the Liberty Ship. Squad by squad, platoon by platoon, the company formed up on the dockside, waiting to board the gangplank on the Liberty Ship and become a part of the armada that stood ready to be launched against the Nazis in the south of France.

"TENNN-HUT!"

Dog Company came to attention aboard the Liberty Ship. They had put out to sea hours ago and milled about on the deck, killing time before the moment when they would be called to action.

"All right you lovin' heroes, fall in!" Sergeant Minnevitch shouted as the company commander, Captain Smilin' Mike Calhoun, came into view. The officer had something to say to his men.

The men called him Smilin' Mike because of a personality trait they had observed. Whenever Calhoun got p.o.'d at somebody, he broke into a broad grin. When that happened, it was time to look out, because Smilin' Mike was about to let go with both barrels.

"Men," Calhoun began, "I want to introduce you to my new second in command. Lieutenant Hank Canfield here is a veteran of the war in Italy and a soldier's soldier whom I know you'll be proud to serve under. Canfield was wounded at Anzio and was decorated with the Medal of Honor. I'll let the lieutenant introduce himself to you doughfoots from here on.''

Buddy Kelso had to fight to keep his jaw from dropping as low as the dragging muffler on the Packard sedan he had left behind in a garage back in Ponca City. He was now looking straight at the rear-guard jockey whom he, Mutt and Haystacks had sandbagged the day before in Naples. His other two buddies hadn't gotten as good a look at the guy's face as he had, so maybe they still didn't realize it was the same officer they'd clocked.

Still, Kelso's Einstein-like intellect told him that there was nothing to get all hot and bothered about, at least not yet. He had made sure that his head was down when he'd come out of the alley. It had only been a split second before Haystacks put the gunnysack over the guy's head. There was no way he could have gotten a good enough gander at him to recognize his mug.

Kelso told himself to just keep his shirt on and not act like a sap, and everything would be just jake. The lieutenant would never be the wiser as long as he didn't give himself away by doing or saying anything dumb. Kelso smiled broadly, baring his toothy grin. Nope. There was no way that Canfield would ever catch wise to the straight dope—of that he was sure as he was of his own moniker.

THE LIBERTY SHIPS set sail in a dull gray flotilla across the surface of a dully gray sea. It was two hours after sunrise, at 0740 hours. The assault on France was scheduled to commence at precisely 0800 hours. The sea was choppy with great rolling swells, and the water changed color as the sky slowly became lit, streaked here and there with bands of red and gold.

On land the enemy spotters manning the coast could suddenly see the Allied assault formation clearly. The surprised Germans were soon wide-awake. Speaking quickly into microphones of radio sets in the manner of frightened men, they relayed the warning of an invasion to the commander of the coastal defenses, who promptly mobilized the Nazi defensive forces. Everywhere along the coast, cursing Germans were grabbing their socks.

The Liberty Ships dropped their Higgins boats within two miles of the landing zones. Dog Company was among the many other assault units that had climbed down the netting and deployed into the LCPs as they rolled in the ocean swells.

The Allied assault force was ready to strike at their targets on the beaches. Already the first waves of Free French Forces were piling into their assigned landing barges. The push to liberate the south of France from the Nazi swastika was on. The Thunderbirds of the Oklahoma National Guard would be leading the coming charge. They would be among the first GIs to hit the beach. They were ready also to be the first combat troops to die.

# BOOK TWO:
# Fields of Fire

Vicinity of Sainte-Maxime, France
August 1944

**5**

*Blue Beach*

Private First Class Dewey Olcott fingered his lucky Indian-head penny and thought fleetingly about home. His back was straight up against the hard iron bulkhead of the landing barge that chugged steadily toward the beach zone some five hundred yards ahead.

Beneath his butt he felt the rumbling of the assault craft's engines. Over his head there was the steady whump! whump! whump! of German flak from inland gun batteries.

Olcott had been carrying his lucky penny since grade school in Muskogee, Oklahoma. He believed that it—and the grace of a merciful God—had been responsible for carrying him safely from North Africa to Sicily and the Anzio bloodbath. Olcott hoped that the same would hold true in the campaign in southern France.

Sergeant Joe Minnevitch was slouched against the gunwale in full battle dress, including entrenching tool, canteen and musette bag containing maps, field glasses and other sundries. Canvas pouches clipped to grommets in the web belt around his waist contained extra .45-caliber ammo for the tommy gun he ported and the Colt M1911 automatic pistol that hung from a leather holster at his right thigh.

Heavy canvas puttees fitted over his combat boots and afforded some protection to his calves and lower

legs, while his bayonet knife was scabbarded just behind his left shoulder, positioned where he could grab
it quickly and either fit it to a rifle or employ it as a
combat knife to stab the enemy in close-quarters
fighting.

Minnevitch sucked the smoke of his Philly cigar
deep into his lungs. Nothing like the sea air and a good
five-cent cigar to get a guy in the right frame of mind
for getting his clock punched, he thought to himself.
He had always wanted to take a trip to the French
Riviera, and these beaches were as damned good a
dying place as anywhere else in this man's war.

The sergeant understood from Smilin' Mike's
briefing on board the Liberty Ship that the enemy was
not entrenched as deeply on these shores as they had
been at Normandy the past June. This development
and the fact that they were on the retreat all over
France meant that the landing promised to be somewhat less risky than the others.

But storming the beachhead wasn't going to be a
cakewalk, though. The Germans wouldn't be throwing rice and confetti. They would be throwing hot,
blazing lead. They had tank support, too, in addition
to Stukas, Messerschmitts and battle-hardened troops
who were no pushovers.

"Get ready to disembark," the LCP's skipper suddenly hollered out above the crashing of the surf and
the deafening din of battle. "See you guys in the funny
papers."

Within the Higgins boat, First Platoon formed up
and made the final checks on their weapons, kissed
religious medallions and fingered lucky talismans and

again thought of a home they were likely never to see again.

The tumult of bolt actions being cocked and ammo clips snapped into the receivers of M-1 rifles came loud above the sounds of bellyaching and prayers, the nervous shuffling of combat-booted feet on the deck of the landing barge and the surge of the surf slapping against the port and starboard flanks of the LCP.

Now shuddering from stem to stern through a storm of flak, the Higgins boat lurched to a stop as its prow hammered against the hexagonal invasion obstacles anchored by German assault engineers in the muddy bottom.

The gut-wrenching jolt of landing was followed by the ratchet and slap of the steel-plate debarkation ramp being dropped to the shallow water, throwing up a cascade of sea foam.

All along the crescent-shaped expanse of French Riviera beach frontage, beneath the overcast skies of a gray midsummer morning, the landing barges bearing the New Minutemen of the Oklahoma National Guard were lowering their ramps.

Railing to the skies as they hoisted their weapons, cursing their fates as they prepared to offer up their lives for the cause of freedom, American GIs readied themselves to pour from the amphibious landing craft and hurl themselves against another enemy beachhead where they would be baptized in steel, fire and blood.

There, just ahead, the enemy waited with weapons trained on the killing ground that was still silent and undefiled.

Dug in among the grass-topped dunes dotting the yellow-white sands of the beachhead, the Germans watched the GIs surge from the landing barges in a cheering, shouting, ya-hooing wave. The Nazis were hunkering behind barbed-wire barricades on the low bluffs that rose twenty to thirty feet on the landward side of the beach.

The battle-hardened Wehrmacht troops of General Blaskowitz's Nineteenth Army were reinforced by crack SS commando units marched hastily to the front from the failed campaign in Italy and also from occupied Belgium.

With their backs up against the wall, the Germans were deadlier than ever. Recently the High Command had suffered a big shake-up. General von Kluge, the original commander of Nazi forces in the north, had been sacked by Hitler only days before because the Führer suspected him of negotiating for surrender to the Allies. The beleaguered Nazis were as prepared to die for their fatherland as they had ever been.

The roaring khaki wave that rushed in through the shallows gained the beach line, advancing well within range of the enemy guns. But still the Germans held their fire. They had been ordered not to open up with their guns until the enemy had gained the beachhead in strength. They would wait patiently until the right moment came.

As it did from the landing craft all along the beachhead, a great tumultuous roar erupted from the Higgins boat that had ferried First Platoon in toward the landing zone from a Liberty Ship anchored offshore. The roar was made up of battle cries spontaneously shouted from a hundred GI throats.

It was a sound that struck fear into the Germanic soul, because the cries of the Americans as they charged into battle was not the orchestrated shouting of the German masses.

This cry was something entirely different. Something the Nazis had never heard before, and a sound that filled them with mortal terror. It was the battle cry of men who were free, men prepared to die so that liberty would not perish from this earth.

CORPORAL JOHNNY AMBOY cussed a blue streak as his right knee buckled and he pitched sideways into the rolling surf. As Amboy went down in the drink, the doughfoot did not hear the crack of a 7.92 mm bullet fired from a Gewehr-43 rifle three hundred yards away, shattering the face of the Thunderbird standing beside him.

The bullet had been meant for Amboy.

Still cursing, Amboy regained his footing. Seawater had gotten up his nose, and his nasal passages were on fire. His eyes had been blinded by the water, too. Amboy felt something blunt and heavy thud against his right shoulder. Turning, he prepared to launch a string of insults at the GI who had shoved him when his back was turned.

"Hol-leee—" Amboy's epithet was cut short as he spotted the corpse of the GI who had been hit. He lay facedown in the surf, his Garand rifle useless beside him.

Amboy felt the vomit rising in his gorge and struggled to keep it down as he pushed his helmet onto his head and turned toward the beach to join the rest of the unit, whose first members were already starting to dig in.

Now the enemy had opened up full kilter on the invaders, pouring automatic fire and raining shrapnel from high-explosive mortar rounds on the GIs in a curtain of death. The Germans had waited to unleash their firepower long enough, and they sprang into action like hungry watchdogs let off their leashes.

As the two dogfaces splashed toward the line of yellow-white sand through the washing surf, Kelso and Haystacks both yelled at the tops of their lungs and cranked fire from their M-1 rifles.

Both doughfoots knew that they didn't have the range to do any damage and that each round they fired used up that much more of the paltry hundred rounds they'd been issued on the Liberty Ships, but it felt damned good and helped dispel the heebie-jeebies.

Kelso hit the beach a fraction of a second before Haystacks did and launched himself at the nearest tussock of sand as he'd done at Anzio last year, flattening himself as much as he could to get the best possible cover against the barrage.

Despite the coppery taste of terror in his mouth and the baneful thunder of the artillery that had just begun in earnest echoing in his brain, Kelso was glad to still be among the living.

Although among the first men out of the Higgins boat, Minnevitch was one of the last GIs to hit the beachhead. Braving the hail of German lead—bullets that he knew were targeted on him by at least one of the gun crews on the bluffs—Minnevitch pushed and shoved his men toward the beach, chewing out those who had halted to try and help dead comrades, pushing along those whose legs were frozen with fear or whose fear was making them turn back toward the landing craft.

Now, as the LCP's machine gunner swung the barrel of the big .50-caliber Browning, chambered his first round and started firing a chattering barrage of answering steel, Minnevitch splashed through the shallows and dashed toward shore.

German lead made frothing spokes of water jump like devils snapping at his heels, but still Minnevitch ran toward the beach, hearing the stutter of the LCP's big .50-caliber gun now joined by the roar of its diesel engines as the skipper turned the craft around and headed full-speed to sea again.

Just then Minnevitch heard the whine of an 88 mm shell as its trajectory brought it over his head. He knew a split second before the round hit that it would land on target. He knew it as surely as he knew his own name.

*BUHHHH-LOOMMMM!*

The Higgins boat disintegrated in a fireball as the direct hit pulverized its steel hull as if it were so much brittle tin. The LCP's crew cried out in mortal agony as human firebrands thrashed in convulsions of death within the lake of burning diesel fuel blanketing the surface of the ocean.

Turning his head, Minnevitch saw the flame-wreathed figures thrash around and sink quickly from view. The poor bastards, he thought. They never had a chance.

Minnevitch kept on running, feeling his heart pump inside his chest as his legs propelled his body forward through space. And then he was dug in on the beach, miraculously still alive and still in one piece, trying to shut off the pictures and the sounds of men being burned alive that spun around and around in his brain like a film loop that he couldn't stop.

**6**

*Green Beach*

A flesh-shredding whirlwind of rotoring Krupp steel crackled from the pillbox built into crest of the low sandstone bluffs overlooking the beach line of the French coast. Pinned down along the bluffs, every dogface in Third Platoon tucked down his head and mashed his nose into the sand, dirt and stone, desperate to avoid catching the round that bore his name.

The German fortifications on the rocky bluffs above the beach line were not as extensive as elsewhere in the war. But the Nazis were ready for anything and determined to give up only after making the Allies pay a heavy price.

The doughfoots of Third Platoon didn't know any of that, and even if they had known, not a man among them would have given a damn. All the GIs cared about was getting their faces out of the dirt and their exposed rear ends out of the line of German firepower raining down on them from the pillbox.

Sergeant Jethro Bullock, the platoon's NCO—or Non-Chickenshit Officer, as he preferred to think of it—wished he had air support available. What the defenders in the pillbox needed was a dose of ten-ton bombs to soften them up. Ah, what sweet music they would make as they screamed earthward and pulverized the blockhouse in a shower of rubble and flame, he fantasized longingly.

Bullock knew that there was no point in trying to reach his company command post, though. The few P-38s available had their hands full strafing units farther inland. Like other Thunderbird platoons strung out along the French Riviera beachhead, his dogfaces were strictly on their own.

Firing their rifles at the poured-concrete blockhouse was quickly using up precious ammo reserves. The platoon's weapons didn't have the range or the penetration power to do any more than pockmark the surface of the pillbox with a zigzagging pattern of bullet holes.

On the other hand, the long ridged black barrel of the VZ37 medium machine gun that jutted from the horizontal embrasure—one of two that gave the pillbox a one-hundred-sixty-degree fire arc on both perimeters—was as deadly a weapon as they came. The MG easily packed the range and the firepower to chew up the whole squad if it made a run for it.

"Surrender at once!" hollered the German commander from inside the pillbox. "You have no chance. You are hopelessly outgunned by the might of the German Wehrmacht!"

To add teeth to their demands for immediate capitulation, the defenders let the Americans have it with another burst from the heavy-caliber VZ37 machine gun emplaced within the pillbox. The wide slit of the gun port cut into the concrete afforded a wide fire arc. Their guns could reach any target between their position and the beach line.

"Surrender!" came the shout again during a lull in the firing. "We give you one last chance!"

"Nuts to you!" the GIs shouted back. "And fuck Hitler while you're at it!"

"To hell with Roosevelt!" the Germans hollered a minute later.

"Nuts to Mussolini, that stinking wop!" taunted the dogfaces in answer.

"To hell with Eisenhower!" the enemy returned, not to be outdone.

"Fuck Himmler and that fat prick Göring!" the GIs countered.

"Fuck Betty Grable!" came the yelled response.

*"Now you're talkin'!"* the dogfaces hollered back finally. At least that was one thing the Germans and they could both agree on.

The Germans had enough of bantering with the Americans and started throwing automatic fire at the dogfaces moments after the final verbal exchange with their enemies.

As they opened up, Wehrmacht troops stationed in the slit trenches that ran around the pillbox joined the barrage on the GIs with Panzerschreck "Tank Terror" rocket launchers.

The German equivalent of the American bazooka—indeed, it was inspired by captured U.S. bazookas—fired a hollow-charge, 7.25-pound warhead packing roughly the equivalent of the bazooka's destructive power, although what the Panzerschreck offered in killing power it gave away in range and accuracy.

Notorious for the voluminous clouds of noxious smoke it produced when fired, the Panzerschreck had earned the reputation as an inaccurate weapon, which explained why the Tank Terror's strikes against the Americans were doing little damage as long as the GIs remained crouched behind secure cover.

BULLOCK HAD ENOUGH of being a sitting duck. Remaining pinned down meant that sooner or later the enemy would clean house with them.

Within the stressed-concrete enclosure of the pillbox, the Nazi stormtroopers were well protected. The Wehrmacht soldiers had plenty of sausage, bread and beer and room to move around within the confines of their underground bunker. They could hold out for a damned long time.

The Americans, on the other hand, exposed and short on ammo, had no such options.

"Yarbrough and Truelove, front and center."

The two-man bazooka team dodged German fire as they sprinted up toward Bullock's position. They had already figured out what Bullock wanted of them, and were itching to try their luck against the pillbox.

"I want you two yardbirds to blow me a pretty hole in that pillbox," Bullock ordered the men. "I want it pretty enough to kiss. You got that?"

"Can I make a pretty hole with this baby?" Yarbrough asked his partner. "Tell the sarge. Go on, tell 'im."

"Sarge," Truelove said, "he ain't just blowin' hot air. He can make you a hole so damned pretty it'll break your lovin' heart. I tell you he's an artist, Sarge. With a bazooka, he's a regular Michelangelo."

"Just make it pretty," Bullock growled, watching Truelove and Yarbrough set up the bazooka through razor-slitted eyes. "Just make it pretty enough to kiss."

Squatting behind Yarbrough, who ported the firing tube on his shoulder, Truelove opened up the canvas ordnance satchel containing six finned bazooka rounds.

Carefully Truelove inserted one round into the rear of the firing tube and hit Yarbrough on top of his helmet with balled fist.

The bazooka roared instantly, ejecting a 2.36-inch high-explosive rocket round through the air toward the German emplacement in a belch of fire and smoke. The bazooka rocket hit the target a little on the low side, exploding in the slit trench directly in front of the pillbox.

But the round had scored a bull's-eye just the same. In the aftermath of the explosion, the air filled with the screams of Germans whose broken bodies and severed limbs were hurled into the air by the force of the blast.

The survivors in the pillbox opened up with sustained machine-gun fire before the stiff sea wind could part the stinking clouds of ordnance smoke, but by then Truelove had slid a second round into the pipe of the bazooka.

A trigger squeeze from Yarbrough sent the high-explosive rocket projectile screaming toward the pillbox on a trajectory that was flat and sure. The well-aimed round hit with a solid bang just to the left of the gun embrasure.

"What did I tell you, Sarge?" Truelove yelled above the sound of the explosion with a laugh as he pounded his fist on Yarbrough's helmet a moment later. "He's an artist. A regular lovin' Michelangelo!"

The third bazooka rocket struck even closer to home. Yarbrough fired another round and then one more at the German pillbox in rapid succession. All of the rounds struck their targets with deadly accuracy.

When the smoke cleared, though, little had changed. Although the Germans in the slit trenches were dead, their greatcoated bodies strewn about like disjointed rag dolls, the pillbox itself remained undamaged.

The only thing that had changed was that Third Platoon was getting dangerously low on ammo and the defenders left in the pillbox were madder and meaner than ever before as they opened up with a fresh salvo of automatic fire. The renewed Nazi attack sent Bullock and his unit scrabbling for cover across the rocky bluffs like ants on the floor of hell, trying to hide from a whirlwind of destruction.

## 7

## Blue Beach

The sound of the explosion that destroyed the LCP that had carried Minnevitch and his dogfaces to Blue Beach had hardly died away when the Germans brought up a Panzer tank.

The Panzers had been deployed in the Mediterranean theater by General Blaskowitz. The veteran officer had learned the lesson of Normandy well.

There, Hitler had been enjoying a holiday at Berchtesgaden, his "eagle's lair" high in the Bavarian Alps, with his girlfriend, Eva Braun. The lodge overlooked the sleepy town of Salzburg, Austria, and the majestic scenery of the Black Forest.

Unable to rouse their Führer from his slumbers, Oberkommando Der Wehrmacht had been forced to stand by helplessly as the Allies established a beachhead.

The Germans had poured withering firepower on the invaders from all directions at once. Field Marshal Erwin Rommel himself had inspected the formidable Atlantic Wall defenses to make certain that they were the most deadly array of fortified emplacements ever used on the field of battle.

The firepower and the fortifications had proved not to be up to the task of withstanding the wave after pounding wave of men and matériel that the Allies had hurled against the German-held shores.

The crack Panzer division would have turned the tide, but only Hitler could release the armor for battle. Hitler had not, and in the end the Germans had been pushed back and an Allied beachhead was secured.

Blaskowitz wasn't about to make the same mistake here in the south. His crack Panzers were deployed along the line of low bluffs fronting the beach, ready to unleash pulverizing firepower on the invaders.

Secured behind camouflage mosquito netting, where they were impervious to attack from the air, the Panzers sat on the highway like an army of giant armored beasts of prey. The moment to deploy them was finally at hand.

The Panzer crew swung the ponderous gun turret in the direction of the platoon of GIs deployed in a thin khaki line behind the dubious cover of the swales and tussocks of beach grass. They lowered the turret, intending to use the guns like field pieces.

The big guns roared, and the shells lobbed from their muzzles whistled through the air, striking their targets with sudden convulsive force.

"HERE THEY COME, SARGE. Wow! Just lookit 'em!"

Private Dunk Corrigan hunkered behind the Browning Automatic Rifle that had been set up on its bipod leg mounts. The BAR man, as well as Minnevitch and every other member of the detail on the beach—mostly First Platoon, but made up of stragglers from other units displaced by the confusion of the landings—sighted the line of gray-coated Germans skittering down the side of the bluff.

"I'd rather be looking at Dorothy Lamour," Minnevitch growled. "I'd rather be looking at anything but heinies."

"They ain't Dorothy Lamour, Sarge," Corrigan answered. "They're krauts. Ugly lookin', goose-steppin', sieg-heilin' katzenjammers. I can see that right off."

"Maybe you're wrong, Corrigan," Minnevitch growled. "Maybe you're really looking at Dorothy Lamour and you don't even know it. Why don't you take another gander?"

"No way, Sarge," Corrigan said a moment later. "It's definitely krauts, Sarge. I just checked again to make sure."

*BUHHHH-LAAMMMM!*

The big round from the Panzer gun sailed overhead, chugging like a freight train before hitting the ground, where it gouged out a crater not more than a couple of feet from the main body of the platoon. So far, big-shell strikes hadn't been the cause of any major casualties. In fact, the shelling had done some good by opening up a bunch of craters in the beach that were being put to good use by the GIs, who hunkered in them for cover.

Now, though, the Germans were sending out their crack Panzer Grenadiers. While the Panzer's big gun and the 7.92 mm machine guns worked by its fire crew blasted out their fiery death knell, the Grenadiers moved down to engage the enemy.

The German infantry troops were armed with Schmeisser submachine guns and Gewehr automatic rifles. They were well trained and easily a match for the hardened combat veterans of the Thunderbirds.

"Come on, you doughfoots! Kick the krauts in the Axis!" Minnevitch roared. At the same time, Corrigan opened up with the BAR. His first salvo dropped two storm troopers, who collapsed facedown in the sand. The rest of the Germans were forced to hit the dirt and tuck in their heads.

Suddenly the Panzer's big gun opened up again. The shell struck, throwing up a cloud of dirt. The GIs were up and firing the instant that the explosion's final echo died away. Now the enemy soldiers were so close that the GIs could see the bayonets gleaming on the ends of their weapons. Some doughfoots fancied they could even see the cold glint of hatred in their eyes.

Private Luke Acuff clutched his throat as his face disintegrated under a burst of parabellum Schmeisser rounds. Hot bright blood fountained from a dozen ragged wounds. Aiming his Schmeisser rifle, the scowling soldier who put him down pumped more Krupp steel into the writhing, twitching body before his gun ran dry.

As the Nazi unsnapped the ammo mag and fumbled for a fresh one, Corporal Johnny Amboy lobbed a hand grenade. "Here, Fritz, have one on me," he shouted. Three seconds later the grenade exploded, blowing the attacker to smithereens.

Again the Panzer roared its fiery bellow of destruction, but the shells had just as good a chance of hitting the Germans as the Americans. The Thunderbirds and the Panzer Grenadiers were engaged in fierce hand-to-hand combat on the sands of the bloody beach.

Like the rest of the platoon, Sergeant Joe Minnevitch lashed out with bare knuckles and the raw, cold steel of his bayonet when his gun ran out of bullets.

Although the beach soon became a dying ground for the Nazi patrol, the Thunderbirds' situation had not changed appreciably. They were still pinned down on the sand, facing off against German armor with little more than iron guts, bare fists, a couple of rifles and a few lousy grenades.

JOE MINNEVITCH pushed his helmet back on his forehead and counted the seconds between the first bang of the shell being fired and the much louder report when it hit and exploded. One, two, three, four, five, six, seven. That would be all the time his men would have to make the run from the beach to the top of the bluffs.

By this time the Germans were in as bad shape as his own guys were, but the enemy had tank support and time was on their side. Minnevitch's troops had to get off the beach right away. If they died, so what? They were all going to die sooner or later, anyway. Minnevitch figured they might as well do their dying on their feet as on their bellies.

"Move when you hear me sound off," Minnevitch shouted. A second later he yelled, "Go! Go! Go!" leading the charge, Minnevitch and privates Stratton and Kelso hustled from their positions.

Stratton got only a couple of feet before a 7.92 mm round cut him down. His broken body was viciously hurled sideways to land in a crumpled heap on the bloody French sand.

His last earthly thought was that he would never get a chance to see the bouncing baby boy his wife, Lorraine, had given birth to the previous month. With that thought still in his mind, he left this life.

Minnevitch and Kelso succeeded in making the dangerous run to the base of the bluffs. There they were temporarily safe from the Panzer rounds and the machine guns.

The Schmeisser-armed German troops also had a tough time of it as they tried to fire down on the enemy from over the ledge of the sandstone bluffs. They kept up a steady stream of cursing as they spit steel and fire at the Americans.

But the sergeant was prepared for the final push. He had collected the last few hand grenades from the unit and ganged them together with electrical tape. He now had three cluster bombs made up of four grenades each.

Minnevitch yanked the pin of the first cluster charge and watched as Kelso did the same. Since Stratton was gone, that would only leave the two dogfaces to deal with the Panzer.

When the Thunderbirds pinned down on the beach opened up with the last few dozen rounds of ammo they had left, drawing the Panzer's fire and making the enemy on the edge of the cliff duck for cover, Minnevitch and Private Kelso jumped out and hurled their grenade clusters.

The clustered charges went off with thunderous bangs, the two explosions merging into a single fierce concussion. Damage to the tank was great because the grenades had rolled beneath the front end of the Panzer. When they exploded, their combined shrapnel and blast penetrated the underside of the Panzer.

Huddling behind some rocks, Minnevitch heard the tank go up and was sure that it was burning as the Thunderbirds leapt from their cover positions and ran hell-bent toward the bluffs, their guns roaring and their voices sounding savage battle cries.

In only minutes they were taking the surviving Germans prisoner. As they spilled from the Panzer, the Thunderbirds stripped them of their weapons and sliced off the top button of each prisoner's pants with their bayonet daggers to discourage their trying to run away. Then the German captives were lined up along the ruins of an old stone wall.

"You know what?" Kelso remarked to Haystacks as he looked over the German prisoners who were holding up their pants.

"No, what?"

"For the master race," Kelso went on, "these krauts ain't so fucking tough. In fact, they got no moxie."

"How do you know that, Kelso?" Haystacks asked. "Maybe they got moxie. Maybe they just don't show it."

"Hey, Fritz," Kelso said, stepping right up to a man whom he'd selected at random. "You got any moxie?"

The man looked at him with frightened eyes and made a gesture that meant he didn't understand. *"Bitte, bitte?"*

Kelso waved his hand disgustedly. "See what I mean," he said as he trudged away, his rifle on his shoulder and a butt between his lips. "No goddamn moxie at all."

## 8

*Green Beach*

"Truelove, how come them krauts are still throwing shit at us? I thought Yarbrough was an artist."

"He's an artist, all right," the private said back sheepishly. "A regular Michelangelo. Them krauts just don't appreciate good art, that's all."

"You got any suggestions, soldier?"

"Yeah, Sarge," Truelove returned. "What we need is to get right on top of that pillbox and lay some demolition charges. New stuff—plastic, it's called. If we place the charges right, the whole emplacement will split open pretty as you please."

Yarbrough might have run fresh out of bazooka shells, but he did have a block of demolition plastic, as well as the detonator caps that went with the stuff.

While the dogfaces of the Oklahoma Guard and the Germans traded fire, Yarbrough set to work making satchel charges using the plastic, detonators, timers and canvas musette bags.

Bullock stuck out his hand when Yarbrough was finished with the satchel charges. He had something to say to the dogface before he went any further.

"This isn't volunteer duty," Bullock informed the GI Joe. "I'm going." Bullock was determined to make the run, but Yarbrough wouldn't have any part of it.

"Uh-uh, Sarge," he replied. "You'd never make it. For one thing you're a lot bigger than I am, and I'm also betting that you're a whole lot slower, too."

Yarbrough was a champion track star in high school. He was probably the only man in the unit who stood half a chance of delivering the satchel charge to the kraut position, he explained.

Bullock didn't like it, but he was forced to see the truth of what Yarbrough was saying.

Turning to take a long, hard squint at the stretch of unsecured beach that had to be traversed, Bullock estimated that something like two hundred yards of rocky, hardscrabble terrain lay between them and the German gun crew.

Yarbrough was right, Bullock realized. He'd never stand a chance of making it. But Bullock also knew as sure as sunshine that Yarbrough would never make it, either.

Okay, he'd maybe get close enough to pitch the charge, but it would take a lovin' miracle for those machine guns not to cut him down before the charge exploded.

"You know what you're getting yourself into, soldier?" Bullock asked. Yarbrough nodded, and Bullock could see by the expression on his face and the determined look in his eye that the buck private knew damned well that the odds were heavily stacked against him.

"Okay," Bullock finally said. "Get moving."

"What did I tell you, Sarge," Truelove said with a grin. "He's a regular artist."

A WORLD OF HOT LEAD thrown by Third Platoon might not have done anything serious to the pillbox, but it forced the Germans to tuck in their heads. Bullock shouted to Yarbrough to haul ass as the unit poured on the firepower.

Carrying the satchel charge, Yarbrough sprinted up toward the pillbox. When the stuttering flashes marking one of the two chattering machine guns pivoted suddenly in his direction, he knew that the Germans had spotted him.

Bullets kicked up chunks of spinning debris as the Germans opened up on the sprinting American. They had seen the satchel charge he was carrying and knew full well that it could wipe them out.

They had to stop the dogface or go to hell in a hurry. It was one or the other. Both guns tracked away from the GI unit pinned down astride the bluffs and throwing diversionary fire. The weapons of the Germans were now trained exclusively on Yarbrough.

"Go, you mother-lovin' jaybird! *Go! Go!*" Bullock hollered at Yarbrough, but in his heart he knew the dogface didn't have a snowball's chance on a hot griddle of making it there and back alive.

Still on the run, Yarbrough dodged German steel, then unexpectedly fell to the side. For a moment it looked as though he'd been hit. Then Bullock saw the thumbs-up sign, and Yarbrough was up again, using the fresh volley of cover fire from Bullock's unit to throw off the Germans' aim.

Closer and closer he got. Yarbrough could see the white gleam of the scowling faces beneath the dull metal of the German helmets. Yarbrough's mind and heart were on fire as he willed his tired legs onward.

But his legs were rapidly turning into lead weights beneath him.

Still he willed himself forward, pushing his body across the open space toward the death-spitting guns, willing his mind to ignore the whine of the ricocheting bullets that slammed into the rubble around him.

At last Yarbrough was almost on top of the pillbox. He could see the heat shimmering as it rose off the white concrete surface, and he could smell the odors of overheated gunmetal and cordite smoke. He could taste the salt of the sea air and the coppery tang of his own fear.

The Germans inside the pillbox were close enough to see Yarbrough, too. They could see the American's face, grotesquely contorted by exertion and pain. They also saw the bundle of death he clutched in his hand.

The Germans knew that they had to stop him before he had a chance to hurl it toward them. With panic now, they sighted on the rapidly advancing soldier, squeezing off burst after burst.

A flash lit up the world. It lit up the world and for a moment Yarbrough seemed to hang in the air, hang there as if he were weightless. But Yarbrough wasn't weightless; he had been struck by the 3-round burst of Nazi steel.

The flash was the scream of neurons in his brain as death lit up his nervous system, and the feeling of weightlessness was the first rush of his soul's liberation into the great unknown and the standing still of time as Yarbrough spilled out of his body in a gush of redness.

But even as he died, Yarbrough remembered the job he had come to do. He stretched out his hand and with a final stubborn cuss let go of the satchel charge.

*KUHHHH-UHHHH-BLAMMMM!*

The satchel charge had gone sailing through the air, tumbling end-over-end. It slammed against the edge of the five-foot-long gun embrasure with a hollow clunk, and then it bounced into the German bunker. Yarbrough had pitched the munitions pack with perfect accuracy.

The satchel charge fell into the embrasure and exploded with a thunderous report that instantly destroyed the pillbox under the blast concussion of the detonating plastic explosive.

The Germans inside died instantly. Shrapnel razored through the air, scything through flesh, shearing through bone. The German soldiers' bodies were ripped to shreds, mangled beyond recognition in the deathstorm of shrapnel that tore through the pillbox.

The Thunderbirds were already up and running toward the bluff, then scaling it and swarming the pillbox. A fusillade of bullets and grenades took care of any survivors.

Sergeant Jethro Bullock cradled Yarbrough's broken body in his tattooed arms. There was a tiny spark left inside the GI's shattered body. Just enough to light up the pain-glazed eyes for one last look at the world he was about to leave forever.

"Did we get them krauts, Sarge?" Yarbrough asked weakly, blood trickling from his lips.

"Yeah, soldier, we got them good," Bullock said, and saw Yarbrough smile and try to lift his hand to give him the thumbs-up. But Yarbrough didn't have enough strength left in him, and his hand fell back, as limp now as the rest of his body was getting.

Gently he laid Yarbrough's broken frame down on the shattered, bloody earth of a foreign land and closed his dead, staring eyes with his thumb and forefinger. Picking up Yarbrough's Garand, he jammed the rifle muzzle-end-down into the yielding sand and hung Yarbrough's helmet over the wooden stock, making a battlefield gravestone for a fallen hero.

**9**

*Sainte-Maxime*

Beneath the incessant boom and thunder of the big naval gun batteries hurling fire from the warships anchored offshore, the mammoth Landing Craft Tank barges carrying Sherman tanks and other mechanized armor continued piling up hardware on the beach. Before very long, U.S. tank crews were ready to deploy into the French coastal town of Sainte-Maxime.

Despite continual shelling of the landing zone by the big railway howitzers that the Germans had emplaced farther inland, away from the fury of the Allied frontal attack, the Führer's forces in southern France had no chance of victory, and they knew it full well.

Reeling under the swift, determined advance of the Free French from the right, and the Americans from the left and center, the German battalions were retreating to secure lines farther north and marching eastward into Belgium and the fatherland itself, where the military supremacy of the Third Reich still held sway.

The Riviera beachhead had been quickly secured by General Patch's Seventh Army, allowing for a buildup of troops and matériel unprecedented in the assault on Fortress Europe thus far.

The heavily armed Shermans were deployed quickly after the assault began and assisted the howitzer batteries in bombarding the Germans still entrenched in the area. Once the enemy had been pushed back from the beachhead, the tanks advanced into the town.

Close behind them marched the infantry. And in its front ranks marched the Oklahoma National Guard.

SERGEANT JOE MINNEVITCH and his Thunderbird detail hustled for cover as the Sherman spit fire and steel from its 75 mm turret cannon.

The narrow streets of the old port town were just wide enough to permit the tanks to maneuver, leaving not enough room on either side for a man to pass. Infantry troops took advantage of that by taking cover behind the track-mounted masses of heavily armored steel, where they would be impervious to frontal attack.

The fragmentation round ejected from the barrel of the Sherman was accurately aimed. With the sound of a train whistle, it barreled through the air in an almost flat trajectory.

Moments later the shell dropped right in the middle of the nest of German machine gunners set up in a small square lying about thirty yards in front of the tank. The machine gunners were well emplaced behind barricades made out of sandbags, and large chunks of bombing rubble formed a secure cordon around their position.

A single gun crew in such a strategic spot could hold out for quite a long time against even the most determined infantry assault. But against the Sherman tanks it was another matter. A single well-placed shell was enough to blow most of the crew to hell and gone.

Even before the billowing clouds of smoke reeking of high explosive could begin to clear, the Sherman rolled and clanked into the square. No longer bottled up in the narrow street, the Thunderbirds came spilling into the square right behind it, their guns belching flame and spitting bullets. Those few German soldiers still alive inside the ruins of the machine-gun emplacement danced like marionettes as hot lead and grenade shrapnel riddled them from head to foot.

Minutes later nothing in a field gray German uniform was left alive in the town square. Having done their part, the crew of tankers turned the big steel war wagon and clanked off across the town to assist other infantry units in the battle to secure Sainte-Maxime. The infantry was now well deployed inside the strike zone. From then on it was up to the dogfaces to do their part.

Minutes after the tank's departure, a new menace appeared. Suddenly, from the ruined buildings surrounding the square, a hail of ricochets from automatic fire keened against the flagstoned pavement.

*"Sniper!"* Minnevitch shouted out, and didn't need to say any more. Around him the Thunderbirds were hitting the dirt, scrambling to take cover from the deadly enemy fire. Squatting down behind the ruined wall that surrounded the fountain at the center of the plaza, Minnevitch scanned the perimeter of the square, intent on locating the position of the sniper.

The sniper was a smart son of a bitch. Up against superior numerical odds, he wasn't about to give his position away that easily. Minnevitch knew that the sniper's best protection lay in his mobility. He would fire a burst, then move quickly to another position before the enemy forces could get a fix on him by sighting on his muzzle-flash.

Fire and move, fire and move. Stick a finger in their eyes, then run like hell.

Sure enough, the next burst of automatic fire came from a direction many yards from the position that Minnevitch had thought the first sniper burst had originated from.

This burst had drawn first blood. Private Mickey Temple had exposed himself out in the open a second too long while peering over the edge of the shell hole in which he and his buddies had taken cover. Before he even knew what hit him, he fell back with most of his upper cranium missing and his precious brain oozing out through the gaping fracture.

"Temple caught it," the call went out across the shattered battle zone. "Pass it along."

"How bad?" Minnevitch asked.

"It don't get any badder, Sarge," came the shouted answer.

Minnevitch turned to Kelso and Haystacks, who were hunkering nearby, their rifles propped on the shattered stone masonry, anxiously scanning the perimeter for their unseen enemy with the determination of cornered, frightened men.

"You two birds cover me," Minnevitch told them both. "I'm going huntin' for kraut."

"Check, Sarge."

Before he made a run for it, Minnevitch looked around for something he could use to draw the German's fire. It was the oldest trick in the book, but it didn't get to be that way for nothing. Picking up a chunk of rubble lying on the ground nearby, he gripped it in one hand and clutched his tommy gun in the other.

Minnevitch hoped that the sniper was the nervous type like a lot of his kind, but if he wasn't, then Minnevitch could wind up dead in a hurry.

As it happened, the German *was* the nervous type.

A burst of sudden autofire shrieked against the flagstones of the square as the German tracked on the object that bounced, rolled and skittered across the plaza. Minnevitch was up on his feet even as more shots rang out behind him, hearing the chattering of his squad's guns aimed in the direction of the sniper's muzzle-flash.

Bullets sang at his boots as the Nazi sharpshooter threw another burst at Minnevitch from a couple of feet beyond where the weapon's muzzle-flash had last appeared. Before the man could get a better fix on the fast-moving target, Minnevitch was inside the rubble of the bombed-out building shell from which the sniper operated.

Pinpoints of light flashed to one side as the sniper fired and bullets thudded into the crumbling woodwork. Minnevitch was already sprinting from his place of concealment, spraying the shadowy interior of the ruins with his tommy and ripping a hand grenade from chest webbing.

"One . . . two . . . three . . ." he counted, pulling the pin and lobbing the grenade in a single smooth movement, then taking cover just as the pineapple went off with an earsplitting bang! on the exact count of four. Minnevitch waited a long, slow beat after the blast died away.

Then he sprang from cover, up and running as he whipped the tommy's barrel from side to side to spray the mocking shadows with bursts of .45-caliber panic fire.

Nothing happened. Nothing at all.

Minnevitch took a hesitant step forward and saw the immobile body of the Nazi sprawled across a mound of rubble. Lying on his side, the Nazi looked for all the world like he had lain down and gone to sleep.

It was only when Minnevitch turned him over that he saw the big spreading red splotch in the middle of the German's uniform. When Minnevitch removed his boot from the Nazi's shoulder, the man flopped over completely and fell on his back with his hands outspread.

Letting out a hiss of tension, Minnevitch allowed the tommy gun to hang in his fist and wiped the sweat of fear and exertion from his brow with the sleeve of his dirty field jacket.

"You okay, Sarge?" asked Private Dewey Olcott a minute later as the rest of the unit came running up to the silent ruins. Minnevitch shook his head to clear it. He was still in one piece, and that was a lot more than he'd expected to happen.

"Nothing that a bottle of gin and a dame with plenty of moxie couldn't fix," he answered groggily.

Olcott laughed, then suddenly made a gargling sound and jumped to one side to crash into a pile of broken furniture. As Olcott jumped, Minnevitch heard the crack of a pistol round that had been fired from behind him.

"Olcott, hey, Olcott!" Minnevitch shouted, bending over the GI's limp body. He could still see a flicker of life in Olcott's glazing eyes. Olcott coughed blood as he reached into his pocket and took something out. His last earthly sight was the gleam of his lucky Indian-head penny. He grinned, then coughed up more blood, and then the bloody grin froze on his face for the rest of eternity.

Elsewhere in the shadowed ruins, the German sniper let the P-38 pistol drop from his hand and clatter dully to the floor. The gun was suddenly the heaviest thing in the world, and the German's eyes were already rolled up lifelessly inside his head.

## 10

Dog Company's Third Platoon had a bunch of trouble dealing with the Nazis who were holed up in the ruins along the waterfront. For the enemy, the bombed-out ruins were custom-made fortifications.

Constant shelling and bomb loads dropped from U.S. planes had been responsible for a great deal of the wreckage. But much of the rubble had been deliberately created by the Germans themselves as a defensive measure. As cover, rubble was much superior to intact structures. It could be better defended and was more resistant to attack.

These waterfront ratzis were deeply entrenched within the ruined and bombed-out superstructure of one of the expensive resort hotels that lined the stretch of prime Riviera ocean frontage.

The Germans were using the field of fire commanded by the hotels to excellent advantage. Neither artillery fire nor aerial bombardment had been successful in dislodging them.

Third Platoon was now faced with a down-and-dirty house-to-house clean-up job. In order to carry it out, the platoon divided up into three-man squads. Each squad was assigned a different sector of the pocket of dug-in Germans. His scythe raised above the battle zone, the Grim Reaper of death waited and watched.

WILKINSON, DUFFEE and Keefe trudged cautiously down a narrow alleyway, alert for booby traps and snipers, walking on eggshells. The invading forces had quickly learned that the rooftops of Sainte-Maxime were infested with snipers who had positioned themselves well to take potshots at the troops.

"I'll take the point," Wilkinson soon sang out, receiving a thumbs-up from his two partners in answer. He had spotted a flicker of movement in one of the buildings up ahead and figured there was a sniper with a gun in there somewhere. "You guys come in behind me. Cover my rear, hear? Them krauts got itchy triggers."

"I read you," said Duffee with a nod.

"Check," said Keefe, whose eyes busily scanned the street.

Duffee and Keefe flanked Wilkinson as he stuck a wooden matchstick in the corner of his mouth, said a quick Hail Mary and cradled his M-1 rifle. Then he ran across a narrow cobbled street to the ruined entranceway of a building that had once been part of a shop frontage with apartments on the second and third floors.

The shattered interior of the demolished building was illuminated by a sorry patchwork of sunlight that filtered wanly down through the exposed beams of the blown-out roof as if even the sun didn't want to shine there. From the big frames of the blown-out windows and the profusion of shattered glass littering the floor, the place must have once been a shop, but there was not a stitch of inventory anywhere to be seen to confirm that.

Wilkinson went through an open doorway at the rear and entered another room. Plaster and lath lay everywhere in ragged heaps. Back there, away from the circulating air on the street, the interior reeked sourly of smoke and dry rot. Rainwater that had swept in through the shattered roof had collected in puddles on the busted floor of what probably had been a comfortable living room not too long before.

As his eyes refocused in the changing light condition, Wilkinson saw a raggedy dirty-faced young boy staring at him with the biggest, darkest, roundest eyes he had ever seen.

"Hey kid—" Wilkinson began. He never got to finish his sentence.

A moment later the goose-stepper standing in the shadows behind the boy flung him aside and jerked the trigger of his Mauser machine pistol over and over again, a snarl of hatred on his lips as a fusillade of blazing death exploded from his weapon.

Riddled with lead, Wilkinson was killed immediately, his body doing a twisted half turn before thudding heavily into the wall. Wilkinson slid down the wall to a sitting position with his lower jaw and throat a raw mass of torn flesh, his black hair soaked through with blood and his right eyeball dislodged from its socket.

For a moment one arm jerked spastically back and forth as nerves continued to fire. It looked as if Wilkinson was saying goodbye to his buddies in Company D.

Duffee and Keefe had dived to one side as soon as they heard the sound of automatic fire.

"Wilkinson!" Duffee shouted into the shadowy interior. "Wilkinson, you okay?"

"He's had it," Keefe said to Duffee, his eyes not on his partner but on the room's interior instead. "Let's get that kraut before we get the same as Wilkinson." Duffee knew better than to linger over Wilkinson. He was gone, and that was all there was to it.

Nothing could bring their buddy back. But revenge—now, that was another matter. Besides, they would be sitting ducks if they didn't make tracks pronto.

Duffee and Keefe caught a flash of motion in a sudden beam of dusty sunlight slanting down from the shattered roof and heard the thump of hobnailed boots crunching rubble as the Nazi gunner dodged into a side room. Duffee got off a burst of his tommy, but the .45-caliber slugs only pocked the woodwork, filling the sunlight with still more dust from a spray of plaster and lath.

Now the little kid was wailing like a human air raid siren, crying his head off. Nearby, Duffee and Keefe spotted the stomach-turning sight of the corpses of a man and a woman in the shadows of the floor, and they knew why the kid was making with the waterworks.

Their throats had been slashed like butchered livestock. Flies buzzed around them, and their discolored bodies were bloated and disfigured by decay to the point where they no longer looked human and looked instead like air-filled balloons. From the appearance of the corpses, they had been dead for at least a day, maybe longer.

Now was no time to minister to the kid, either. Duffee and Keefe went after the sniper, catching up with him as he dodged into a doorway and down stairs that led to the basement. Whirling on his heels at the bottom, he cranked off two shots from his Mauser, now on single-fire to conserve ammo.

The 7.63 mm bursts forced the two GIs back against the wall at the doorway's left and right. They pulled hand grenades from chest webbing and lobbed them. The waffled antipersonnel munitions thudded down the wooden stairs like the feet of disembodied ghosts.

Thunk, thunk, thunk...

*KAAAA-BLOOOOM!*

The Nazi was killed instantly by the shrapnel splinters that sprayed across the blast zone in a lethal shower of jagged steel. Duffee and Keefe pushed back their helmets in gestures of relief as they surveyed the damage and made sure that the sniper was really dead. From upstairs, the sound of the kid's crying continued to fill the bloodstained ruins.

Keefe tried giving the kid a chocolate bar from his K-rations. The orphan threw the candy down to the floor and would not shut up for love or money. Then they remembered Wilkinson and went back to their buddy's corpse.

He was still where they had left him and already growing stiff. They snapped his dog tags off his neck and his St. Christopher medallion, too, and they got out his wallet and personal effects. Inside the wallet were photos of his wife and kid, whom Wilkinson would never see again.

SQUAD B FOUND ITSELF up against German units operating in the twisting streets that ran perpendicular to the beachfront. The troops had booby-trapped the streets with makeshift antipersonnel devices to delay the Americans' advance as long as possible.

As he walked down one such street, Private Bill Prouty stumbled across a trip wire that he hadn't seen. Stretched tautly across the street, the transparent nylon cord was almost invisible. One end was tied securely around the base of a fire hydrant, while the other was looped around the pull rings of four stick grenades taped together to form a cluster charge.

To amplify the lethal effect of the grenade shrapnel, the grenades were sitting inside a keg of nails. When Prouty tripped the detonation wire, he simultaneously pulled the pins on the cluster charge and armed the bomb.

Nearest to the booby trap, Prouty barely had time to scream before the cluster of grenades went off. Taking the brunt of the blast and shrapnel, he crossed the thin red line between consciousness and eternity in a split second. His death was mercifully quick and painless, although after being ripped apart by a few hundred nails and shrapnel he was not too pretty to look at.

No such luck for the rest of the detail. They did not even die pretty. The miniature hurricane of flying metal shards reached Prouty's buddies Webb and Farmer a pulse beat later, ripping through their bodies as though they were figures made out of bloody mud. By the time the smoke cleared, there wasn't even enough left of them to bury.

SQUAD C WAS CLOSING in on Nazi positions situated within the ruins of one of the expensive hotels adjacent to the marina. Before the war the French Riviera resort town was one of the playgrounds of the Continent's rich and sophisticated set.

Even with its chairs and tables in disarray and sunlight streaming dustily through the huge gaps in the bombed-out roof, the grand ballroom still bespoke of a magnificent era of elegance and class.

But the Nazis were not its usual occupants. For a moment after the GIs entered the spacious room, the silence was as finely stitched as a shroud of lace. Then, without warning the Germans opened up with a sudden flurry of Schmeisser fire that sent the squad scurrying back toward the entranceway for the cover of the debris littering the hotel lobby.

Fitting M-17 rifle grenades to their weapons, the squad shouldered their guns and fired into the hotel's grand foyer. As the ballroom burst into flames with a roar like the thunder of hell itself, the squad followed through with a volley of massed rifle fire. By the time the fireworks died down, nothing was left alive inside the ballroom.

Just for good measure, one of the dogfaces fired the last rounds in the mag of his M-1 in a final burst. "Shave and a haircut," he shouted above the chattering of his gun, "two cents."

## 11

Street by street, house by house, and mile by bloody mile, the khaki wave of Thunderbirds slowly backed the hard core of the harassed German garrison into a corner from which there was no escape. Paying a heavy toll in casualties of their own, the Oklahoma Guard had advanced swiftly into the center of Sainte-Maxime by the end of the first day of fighting.

With Wehrmacht foot soldiers surrendering by the score, battle-hardened elite units wound up floundering in a pocket ringed on all sides by a cordon of GIs. There was no escape from the pocket, but the Germans didn't give a damn.

The ratzis in the trap were mostly SS storm-troopers who had sworn a fanatical devotion to their Führer and his twisted cause. As long as their deaths were glorious, they preferred being killed in action to being taken prisoner.

The center of the Sainte-Maxime pocket was the town's opera house, a large and ornately ornamented building dating back to the time of Louis IVX. The Germans used the opera house as their center of operations both because of its strategic location and because it had served as headquarters for both the Gestapo and the SS.

A line of fortifications completely encircled the opera house. The barricades included barbed concertina wire strung on iron posts hammered into the ground, sandbag defenses, tank traps and armored cars with their guns trained on access points. Behind these were trenches manned by Germans packing automatic rifles and Schmeisser SMGs.

The Gestapo headquarters contained a veritable arsenal of weapons. Its underground cellars had been redesigned by German army engineers to be completely bomb proof. They served as dungeons and air-raid shelters alike.

Not even a direct hit by howitzer fire could dislodge troops committed to making their final stand from such well-defended ground. If the Nazis were determined to fight it out to the last man, then they could.

The Gestapo and the SS had originally installed barricades to protect themselves against bombing attacks by the French Maquis. The underground was fond of staging daring raids against the hated enemy. In a manner different from the SS, Adolf Hitler had given the French resistance a cause that they too were willing to die for.

Two months before, after the Normandy invasions and Allied troops overrunning most of northern France, the Germans had increased their fortifications in Sainte-Maxime with an eye toward hampering the offensive by troops, as well as mechanized armor. The opera house was now ringed by a defensive maze that the Germans hoped would be impregnable.

Fanned out around the large square that fronted the opera house, flattened in doorways on either side of the narrow streets and alleys that fed into the square like the crooked spokes of a broken wheel, the Thunderbirds traded fire with German storm troopers in the square and around the opera house as they massed for the final assault on the Nazi headquarters.

The Oklahomans still had this one final obstacle to overcome before the battle-weary guardsmen could consider the town secure. However, the opera house was the deadliest challenge they had faced by far in Sainte-Maxime. Not only, they knew, because of its defenses, but also because of the hard-bitten troops within, who were determined to make their final stand and die for their Thousand Year Reich.

SS MAJOR SCHATZKAMMER was the officer in charge of the Nazi holdouts in the opera house pocket. The Sturmbannführer was tall and slim, with the delicate hands of a concert pianist or a brain surgeon and the cold psychotic eyes of a murderer. The major professed a love of opera music, and apart from the purely strategic value of the opera house, had personally selected it as a base because of that fact.

Schatzkammer had gone to Berlin to study medicine, but the tide of the Nazi uprising had changed his plans forever. Completely swept up in the movement, he had become mesmerized by the torch-lit martial parades, the savage drumbeat of jackboots marching across cobbled streets and the romantic promises of heroic death and glory made by Adolf Hitler, a man whom he worshiped and considered the divinely inspired deliverer of the German nation.

In short order he'd been wearing the coveted black uniform of Heinrich Himmler's Schutzstaffel, or SS, and Schatzkammer had taken an oath to spill his blood for the greater glory of Nazi Germany. It was an oath he took as seriously now as he'd done on the day of his initiation into the secret rituals of the SS. If his destiny was to die in the service of his Führer and his country, then he would meet death like an Aryan, fearlessly and even joyously.

There had been some among the holdouts in the opera house who had advocated surrender to the Americans. They had forgotten that Schatzkammer was a devout Nazi. To even breathe the word "surrender" was to disgrace the Führer and the great and glorious cause they had sworn their sacred allegiance to.

A crack of Schatzkammer's P-38 pistol, and the voices of the cowardly dissenters were silenced forever in a torrent of traitors' blood. In the aftermath of the executions there were no other voices raised to join the witless *schweinehund* who had dared to utter the forbidden words of defeat.

Now Schatzkammer barked orders to his SS troops as they hustled to man the access points of the opera house. He had no intention of giving an inch to the accursed Americans without a fight. Yes, they would eventually overrun his position, but they would have to pay a great price for their victory.

The German Führer had ordered all officers to hold every inch of ground unto their death. Delaying the Allied advance as much as possible, bogging it down to give the beleaguered German army a chance to regroup and entrench its positions farther eastward, was not only Schatzkammer's mission—he saw it as his sacred duty as an officer of the Nazi SS.

*"Herr Sturmbannführer!"* his adjutant informed him as he stood glaring from one of the tall windows

of the opera house, seeing the American GIs encircling his position. "The Americans are outside. They have brought up tanks and other armored vehicles."

"Then fire on them, you dolt!" Schatzkammer barked. "Fire on them and don't stop until the last soldier stands. We are Germans! Through our veins there courses the blood of the pagan warriors of old! We cannot and will not allow these degenerate mongrel dogs to march us away as prisoners. We would rather die first!"

*"Jawohl, Mein Kommandant!"* the adjutant shrieked in answer, his eyes bugging at the pep talk he'd been given. "I will make sure the men understand the sacred duty that awaits us, *Mein Kommandant!"*

*"Heil Hitler!"* Schatzkammer bellowed, jutting out his arm and extending his hand palm-up.

The adjutant clicked the heels of his jackboots together and *heil*ed Schatzkammer back even louder. He spun around smartly and raced from the presence of his leader, his brain swimming with visions of the glorious warrior's death that awaited him on the field of battle.

Shaking his head, Schatzkammer waited until the rapid crack of hobnailed jackboots against the floor died away and the room was silent. What a fucking ass Klaus was, he thought. With tin soldiers such as he, no wonder Germany was losing the war. Once again Schatzkammer parted the thick blackout drapes covering the high window and peered down into the street.

The sounds of sporadic firing suddenly built to a crescendo as the boom of a Sherman tank joined the chorus of destruction. The opera house rocked to its very foundations as the shell struck within the defensive perimeter, tearing a gaping hole in the Nazi lines. A sneer tightened across Schatzkammer's face as he watched Klaus the adjutant shout orders and SS troopers rush to close up the gap, many of them falling midstep as American shrapnel or bullets tore through them.

*Dummkopf.* The SS major had seen enough. He let the drapes fall back into place and turned from the window. There was much to be done and little time to do it.

Rushing from his office, the commandant of the opera house strode past the troops manning the last bastion of the Nazis in Sainte-Maxime, returning the salutes of the doomed men with ashen faces who raced past him while the thunder of exploding ordnance blew the glass from the window frames and made the entire building shake.

Finally Schatzkammer reached his destination. In the dungeon beneath the opera house, a steel door led to a walled-off passageway that dated back to medieval times. Only the commandant had the key to this door. Opening, then shutting the door behind him, Schatzkammer was swallowed by darkness. Stooping, he felt in the darkness for the flashlight he had secreted there two months before, when the first reports of the Normandy invasions reached him.

At that time Schatzkammer had realized that Germany was destined to lose the war. Like many other SS officers across the scattered outposts of the Third Reich's Nazi empire, the major immediately made his escape plans. As the heart and soul of the Nazi movement, the SS would be indispensable to the survival of the Nazi dream after the war that must and would end, he was convinced, with the fatherland's defeat at Allied hands.

Playing the beam of the flashlight over the walls and turning his head to make sure he had not been followed, Schatzkammer found the iron strongbox hidden in a niche behind loose foundation bricks. Inside the strongbox were civilian clothes and expertly forged papers giving him an entirely new identity. There was money, too. Thousands in francs, German marks, American dollars and universally negotiable gold coins.

Hiding his SS uniform in the niche and hurriedly changing into the civilian clothes, Schatzkammer shoved the barrel of his P-38 pistol into his waistband and pushed aside a stack of old dusty crates concealing the entrance of an escape tunnel.

As he entered the tunnel, beginning the first leg of a journey that would eventually lead to Switzerland and freedom, Schatzkammer could hear the sounds of American voices as the Allied forces swept into the opera house to round up those of his soldiers who had not yet had the honor to die for their people, their fatherland and their sacred German Führer.

## 12

*Berlin, Germany*

Adolf Hitler, the supreme ruler of the German Nazi Reich, glowered over the map spread on the table before him. Deep in thought, he stroked his famous Charlie Chaplin mustache.

The Führer was in his spacious office located in the Reich Chancellery, its floor-to-ceiling windows overlooking the Unter den Linden—the center of German culture—which Hitler had loved since his days as a failed art student from Austria.

The floor he stood on was sumptuous marble polished to an almost blinding sheen. It was a far cry from the creaking wood planks of the cold-water flat where he had formulated the plans that would topple the doddering kaiser and the Weimar government from power and install the National Socialist, or Nazi Party, in their place.

Surrounded by his chiefs of staff, who waited on his every word, Hitler scanned the map in a silence so complete that those encircling him hardly dared to breathe.

The flesh of his face was slack, and his hollow eyes glittered like wet black stones. But his mind was sharp, cunning. It was focused on the battle for France with the same obsessive concentration that the officers of the General Staff had seen a hundred times before. At such moments it was sheer madness to do or say or even think anything that might disturb Hitler.

Men had paid with their lives for such infractions. Jodl, Manteuffel, Keitel and the rest of the field marshals in the command center looked on in respectful silence as their Führer pondered his next moves.

The stinking traitor von Kluge had been recalled to Berlin, thought Hitler to himself. The *schweinehund* had swallowed a cyanide pill en route, however, cheating the hangman.

It had been better for the traitor that way, much better than the fate awaiting him once he would have arrived in Berlin. Hitler had suspected von Kluge of attempting to forge a separate peace with the accursed Allies.

Von Kluge's cowardly actions had borne out suspicions that the Nazi Führer had been harboring for a long time. Hitler would have hung the traitor from piano wire, as he had done with the treacherous dogs who had tried to kill him at the *Wolfsschanze,* or "Wolf's Lair"—his complex of wooden huts and concrete bunkers in a forest near Rastenburg, East Prussia—the previous month.

Model was one of the few within an ever-growing circle of fools, traitors and spies whom he felt he could trust to at least some degree. The field marshal was one member of the cadre of senior military officers who could still be considered loyal to him and the Nazi cause.

Model would hold his ground until he was relieved or ordered to retreat. Of that, Hitler was as certain as he could be of anything in these trying times.

Model would simply have to hold. If not, then disaster for Germany was assured. So swift and so deadly had been the sweep of the invading Allies across the spine of southern France that his forces had been pushed back at an alarming rate.

At this very moment, the American General Patch's Seventh Army was advancing along the Rhône. There wasn't much to be done in the south. With the Free French Forces also gaining ground in their drive toward the heart of the country, and Blaskowitz retreating from the south, the battle would soon be lost unless something happened to turn the tide of battle in favor of the German nation.

One slim chance, slim as the margin between life and death, remained for the Führer. Hitler's forces were now concentrated in a small enclave around the French mountain village of Falaise. Hitler could see from his map that there was a narrow corridor in this region through which his military men were moving heaven and earth to shuttle troops and matériel with the ultimate destinations of Belgium and Germany.

Still secure, the safe cordon would only hold out so much longer, however. Patton's Third Army was driving toward the east, then turning north, and in only a little while the German forces still remaining in the pocket would be trapped like fish in a drying-up pond, able to be destroyed or scooped up whenever the victors chose to do so. But they were vital to the future, and all effort should go into saving them.

The outcome was up to Model now. Even as Hitler scanned the battle map, the desperate plan to hold the advancing forces at bay until most of his vital troops and supplies could withdraw from France via the secure cordon took shape in his mind. It was a daring plan, and one that only the bravest and boldest could hope to carry out.

Hitler picked up a phone. "Give me Model!" he shouted into the mouthpiece, his voice amplified by the vast chamber. In minutes he was connected with the field marshal, barking out his orders and punctuating them with gestures of his clenched fist like a mad conductor leading an orchestra of the damned.

COLONEL BARNEY HACKETT sat at a desk, before the huge tactical map on the wall of the grand château that served as Thunderbird headquarters in the French coastal town of Sainte-Maxime.

Most of his Thunderbird troops were on thirty-six-hour leave for the moment, but the fighting was bound to escalate in intensity before long.

From forward observation posts at the front lines, encouraging Intelligence concerning the sweep and range of Allied forces against the Germans continued to pour in. The way it looked, the Germans were retreating on all fronts.

It was a refreshing change from the manner in which previous invasions had progressed. The Allies had gotten bogged down by the Germans in Italy. First, after Salerno, due to their own stupidity, then at Anzio, where they'd been too gun-shy to move on Rome, and got bogged down again.

Maybe this time it might not have to go that way. Maybe they could win one hands-down for a change.

The map behind Hackett was festooned with colored pins indicating the ever-changing positions of Allied and German forces. From a glance at the map, it was immediately apparent that great gains had been made by the Allied shock troops in only a very short span of time.

"Here's the crux of the situation of it as I view it, General," Hackett said, addressing the U.S. Seventh Army's commander, General Patch. Hackett swept his hand across the map, indicting the broad scope of the Allied advance into France.

"The worst thing we can do is to allow our forces to lose the momentum they've gained. Luck and determination seems to be on our side for once. We should press the advantage and roll forward with everything we have, in my opinion."

"I agree," the general told Hackett. "But I'm not sure of the timing. What if we advance too quickly and spread our forces too thinly? I just don't trust the Germans. They've tricked us before."

"Sir, we committed the sin of overcaution back in Italy," Hackett countered. "We stormed the beachheads and could have taken Rome in three hours. Instead, we dug our heads in the sand and gave the Germans a chance to burrow in. Let's not do it again. I still say we should push on."

General Patch looked up and considered the battle map on the wall, his keen mind mulling over the problem. He knew that what the colonel had been saying had a great deal of merit, but his instincts argued against a hasty move. Still, it would be the chance to reap great rewards from their advance.

"Okay, Barney," he told the colonel with a nod. "How do you want to work it?"

The colonel smiled.

"Got it all figured out," he responded. "A rapidly moving task force built around the nucleus of the 179th Regiment. At battalion strength, the force punches up through the spine of France and strikes deep into the German lines."

"I see," the general returned. "And then the Germans are neutralized while the rest of our forces strike hard and mop up the rest."

"Precisely, General."

About an hour after their discussion, Hackett's paperwork was interrupted by someone who rapped once on the door. The door opened, and an aide showed a Thunderbird in khaki fatigues inside.

"You wanted to see me, Colonel?"

Colonel Hackett looked up and nodded, consulting the clock on the wall. Captain Smilin' Mike Calhoun was prompt, as usual. Of course, Hackett expected nothing less from his men.

Colonel Hackett explained how he was to command the brigade that was to strike hard, fast and deep into enemy lines. Smilin' Mike listened and took a few notes. He saluted smartly as he left the colonel's office, already turning over mission plans in his head.

AT 2305 HOURS the Thunderbird infantry column that had formed up in the debarkation area behind Allied lines at Sainte-Maxime moved out of the secure zone.

Under cover of darkness the task force began slogging its way in a northeasterly direction that was to eventually take the GI spearhead directly into the German zone of operations.

Burnt cork smeared on the men's faces cut the giveaway glare of reflected moonlight to a bare minimum. The troops were under orders to maintain strict silence, nor were they permitted to light up cigarettes without the permission of their CO.

The two jeeps rode with headlights taped to avoid detection by enemy airborne or ground-based patrols. They served as mobile command stations for the officers leading the task force.

By first light the column was already well beyond the safety of its own lines.

# BOOK THREE:
# Behind Enemy Lines

Occupied France,
August 1944

**13**

*Sector Charlie, Southern France*

Task Force 179 had advanced a great distance north-ward along a corridor that appeared to be devoid of any trace of enemy activity.

Weighed down by full packs containing field rations, entrenching tools, bedrolls, shelter halves and personal effects, the column of Thunderbirds was preceded by a motorized scout unit consisting of a jeep and a motorcycle to reconnoiter the area ahead.

The only other vehicles supporting the patrol were two jeeps that served as command vehicles. These kept pace with the advancing column at all times. The second jeep was outfitted with a .50-caliber Browning mounted on a post in its rear, and was assigned to keep watch on the flanks of the infantry column.

The first jeep was for the personal use of Captain Calhoun and Lieutenant Hank Canfield, who were the TF's commanding officers. Apart from the jeeps, the only form of transportation available was the locomotive power of hundreds of GI dogs stomping through the mud and pounding the asphalt of the mountain roads they traveled.

"Looks like the sun will come out before long," Smilin' Mike remarked to the lieutenant as they rode abreast of the first men in the column of Thunderbirds slogging up the mountain road that climbed steeply through forests of spruce, hemlock and pine.

"Not if the krauts see us first, it won't be," the lieutenant replied. He inhaled the forest air deeply. The dense woods, canopied by branches thick with rustling leaves, still scented the air with summer. It would be several weeks before the leaves began to change color with the onset of autumn.

The smell in the air reminded Canfield of the farm country he had come from just outside of Muskogee, Oklahoma. His folks would be getting ready to bring in the harvest at about this time, he suddenly recalled in a flash of poignant memory.

For a moment the lieutenant's thoughts went far away from the steadily climbing road in the south of France and traveled some three thousand miles back to the Oklahoma farm country he'd come from.

There were drive-in movies where he could watch guys like Gable make out with swell dames like Veronica Lake, and the music of Glenn Miller, and then there was his ma's mouth-watering home cooking. Hickory-smoked bacon and fresh eggs sunny-side up for breakfast, corn fritters and Mission Orange pop for lunch and steak for dinner with apple betty for dessert. Now that was really living.

But then Canfield suddenly remembered again where he was, and his smile vanished from his face in the blink of an eye. His heart pumped furiously, his dogs ached from a touch of trench foot, and the cigarette dangling out of the corner of his mouth tasted like leavings scraped from the floor of hell. The odds of his getting back to that rural town in Oklahoma were small. Too damned small to even be considered genuine.

And if he ever got back alive again, and unmangled by German steel as he had seen hundreds of men before him, could he fit in to society again? Could he ever go to the movies or listen to the big-band music he used to enjoy or do any of the other things that men unscathed by the horrors of war take for granted? The lieutenant didn't think so. Not after what he'd seen and done and suffered.

Marching at the front of the column, a Thompson SMG cradled in his arms, Sergeant Joe Minnevitch was wary and alert. Minnevitch's battle-trained eyes scanned every inch of the road and environs for indications of the enemy's presence.

Although he could hear the sounds of birds warbling in the branches of the trees overhead and felt the fragrant summer breeze wafting across his face, Minnevitch was not about to allow himself to forget for a moment that he was a foot soldier in a dirty and desperate war.

And if he still entertained any illusions about the name of the game, the sound of distant thunder came sporadically out of the north to remind him. The rumble of artillery batteries dueling it out for the right to plant the flag of either liberty or death on French soil came rolling like summer thunder across the hills and valleys. Fierce fighting still held sway in the north, where the majority of Allied and German forces were concentrated.

So far, there had been no sign whatever that enemy patrols were present in the area. For that matter, there was no indication of any other German presence in the corridor through which the U.S. strike unit marched on its mission of search-and-destroy.

The only signs of Hitler's minions were the occasional Storch scout planes that came buzzing overhead every now and then, appearing to float like giant swastika-emblazoned dragonflies on the warm mountain breezes.

There was no mistaking the danger presented by the scout planes, though, and when the Storch announced its presence with the drone of its engine reverberating off the mountainsides, the battalion would immediately dive for cover until the sound of the plane's motor had died completely away.

The tranquility of the forest was deceptive. The situation could change drastically at any moment to one of blood and fire and steel. In fact, as far as Minnevitch was concerned, it was only a matter of time before that happened.

Suddenly Minnevitch heard the telltale drone at the very limits of hearing range that told of a Storch's imminent approach. A moment later Minnevitch hollered for the men of the patrol to take cover.

The shouted warning was passed down the line, and the khaki-clad soldiers disappeared into the big ditches at either side of the road with practiced speed. Nobody wanted to be the man to give away the unit's position by moving too slowly.

All it would take to turn this mountain Eden into a high and bloody hell was a single radio message from the aerial spotter pilot to send in artillery or Stuka dive-bombers.

The TF was lightly armed and designed as a surprise, mobile strike force using shoulder-fire weapons. The benefits of mechanized transport and heavy arms had been sacrificed for stealth and speed, which meant that they would be sitting ducks for any real trouble that the Germans sent their way.

One hundred feet above the tops of the tall trees dotting the sun-washed ridge line, the Storch pilot peered down through his cockpit window. His practiced eyes scanned the mountain terrain for any of the telltale signs that would advertise the presence of enemy troops.

The pilot detected nothing. Not the flash of light from a wristwatch, nor any sign of troop movement among the trees. The Storch passed directly over the heads of TF 179, buzzing and droning in the sun, the pilot believing that all was still and peaceful in the wooded hills below.

"Okay, all clear!" Minnevitch sang out when the last echoes of the Storch's single engine had finally faded into the distance. As the men fell out, the captain decided that this stretch of forest was a good place to take a break. Dogtrotting off the road, the men gratefully fell out on the forest floor littered with pine needles and leaves and smelling of earth and resin.

PRIVATES MUTT Babcock and Buddy Kelso were slumped against the trunk of a big old tree. Mutt had gotten out a V-Mail blank and was writing yet another love letter to Rita Hayworth.

Kelso was reading the funny papers that had come halfway across Europe in his field pack. The stuff was a year old, and he'd read it hundreds of times. But every time Kelso looked at the funny papers, he still found it a treat, maybe just because it meant that he was still alive and kicking.

The pages of newsprint were practically rubbed raw from reading, and Kelso had almost memorized every single word and image, but he was raring to read them through again.

Kelso started as he always did, with Dick Tracy. Sam Ketchum was cornered by Flat Top and about to get it in the belly. Could Tracy save his loyal sidekick in time? Flash Gordon was in the middle of rescuing Dale from Ming the Merciless, and Little Orphan Annie was siccing The Asp on some nefarious Nazi spies who had tried to do in Daddy Warbucks.

As Kelso read the battered funny papers from home, he spooned garbage that was supposed to be real food from a C-ration tin clamped firmly between his legs. What was supposed to be franks and beans tasted like franks and dogshit.

Man, oh, man. What he wouldn't give for some real food. The kind he used to get at the Acme Diner in Ponca City. If Kelso were there right now, he'd order himself up one of their super cheeseburgers with the works, including relish, bread-and-butter pickle chips and crinkle-cut French fries on the side.

He'd wash down the whole thing with a cup of fresh, hot, steaming java and top it off with a gigantic hunk of cherry cheesecake just dripping with whipped cream. Kelso could practically hear the burger sizzling on the griddle and smell the coffee perking in the big stainless-steel urn they had at the Acme.

Mutt began writing, putting pencil point to paper.

Dear Rita,

I am writing to you from the south of France. So far, no enemy action to report. Hope we can meet sometime when I get back Stateside. I ain't no Gable, but I sure know how to make time with a swell jane like you. Maybe I'll catch you in a U.S.O. show. Anyway, have to sign off for now. Got to kill me some more krauts. Also got to break me a few French girls' hearts.

Mutt marked his letter S.W.A.K. and licked the V-Mail envelope and put away the envelope in the pocket of his olive drab field jacket. Other Thunderbirds were also using the rest break to write letters. Usually these were to wives and sweethearts back in the States. Unlike Mutt, most dogfaces liked getting their mail answered.

A couple of GI Joes were clustered around an Oklahoman who sat with his back against a tree and sang softly to himself. A preacher's son was thumbing through the worn pages of a pocket Bible, while his buddy looked longingly at the Kodak snapshot of his girl, which she had given him on the day he left for basic training. The son of a farmer looked at the dry earth and wondered what kind of crops would grow there, while a doctor's son could think only about what it must be like to be buried in such a far-off place.

Most of the men, doing as Kelso was doing, had already gotten out C-rations and were chowing down on chipped beef, American cheese and other food items, pretending that the foul Army grub was really their girl's or their ma's or their favorite diner's home cooking as they scarfed it down. They knew that just like manna from heaven, if Army chow was eaten fast enough, it could damned near taste like anything.

Before too long Smilin' Mike Calhoun checked his chronometer. It was 0842 hours and the men had been taking a rest break for twenty minutes already.

Reluctantly he would have to give the order for the men to fall in and move out.

Rest was a good idea, but it had to be doled out in the proper amounts. Give an enlisted man too much or too little, and he quickly became either lazy or too exhausted to count for much in a firefight.

"Tenn-huttt!" Sergeant Minnevitch's gruff voice boomed through the forest. "All right you yardbirds! Lift 'em up and move 'em out!"

Moments later the column was on the march again, griping and bitching and cussing but determined to go on, come hell, high water or German steel.

## 14

The farmstead was situated in a shallow mountain valley a couple of miles from the woods beside the road where the battalion had bivouacked briefly that morning. It was now 1215 hours, and the men had been on the march without stopping through the steadily rising mountain countryside.

"Minnevitch, front and center," Lieutenant Canfield hollered out to the sergeant. He had a map spread out on the engine cowl of the jeep.

On it, Minnevitch could see, was marked the location of a farmstead only a little way away from their position. The three-man patrol attached to the unit had proceeded ahead in their jeep and motorcycle to recon the area but had not yet returned. That didn't mean that they had necessarily met up with the enemy. In this man's war any number of things could have happened, but it wasn't a good sign, to say the least.

"I want you and Kelso to go and take a gander at that farm," Canfield told them. "See if it looks okay."

"Yes, sir," Minnevitch returned in a tone of voice that most officers didn't like.

Minnevitch wasn't happy with the disappearance of the patrol and figured it was more than coincidence. Things had been going too well. The odds were that the hammer was about to drop real soon. If it were up to him, Minnevitch would skirt the farmstead altogether.

Trouble was, he couldn't proceed just on instinct alone. He knew that he had to have something concrete to tell his commanding officer.

Taking Kelso with him, Minnevitch broke free and left the infantry column. Together they hunkered the final few hundred yards toward the edge of the woods. From that vantage point they could get a good look at the farmstead.

Lying prone in a thicket of underbrush, Minnevitch got out a pair of binoculars and gave the place the once-over. Except for its red clay roof, the farmhouse was constructed entirely out of stone, in the Mediterranean style favored in the southern part of France.

At first glance the place appeared entirely deserted. Through its glassless windows, nothing could be seen to move. On closer inspection Minnevitch could see clearly that the farmstead had been badly damaged in a recent shelling.

Part of the roof was missing, and pieces of farm machinery lay rusting in the yard out front. To one side of the house was a barn and a small paddock with one side of its wooden railing missing.

The farmstead was encircled by untilled fields that should have been alive with growing things by this time of year. Instead, they were overgrown with wild thistle, dandelions and other weeds. Here and there, tall haystacks dotted the landscape.

There was an orchard over by the right with trees heavy with unpicked fruit, though. When Minnevitch scanned the ground, he could see that much of the late-summer crop of fruit had fallen to the ground, where it lay rotting.

Minnevitch handed the field glasses to Kelso. "Take a squint and tell me how it looks to you," he told the private while he chewed on the stub of the cigar between his teeth. As Kelso swept the binocs from side to side, Minnevitch glanced around him. He hadn't gotten himself rid of that bad feeling he'd had before, but he still couldn't put his finger on anything concrete.

"Place looks clean as a baby's butt, Sarge," Kelso said when he was through. "But I dunno, something isn't right."

"Feel the same way," Minnevitch said, chewing on his cigar. "But that won't cut no ice with the lieutenant or the captain. Unless we've got something concrete to tell them, they'll march the unit in."

Minnevitch took the binoculars from Kelso and scanned the farmstead again, looking for signs of concealed Germans he may have missed before. Although he still didn't notice anything that looked wrong, Minnevitch knew that appearances could be deceptive.

After all, his own unit had fooled the German spotters enough times with their hide-and-seek tactics without half trying. The Germans, it was entirely likely, could be playing a similar game with them right now.

SMILIN' MIKE CALHOUN carefully considered what Minnevitch told him. In the end he decided to march the troops directly across the farmstead.

Making a detour around the farmstead merely on the strength of Minnevitch's hunch would amount to gambling with the advantage of speed and surprise, which was his unit's greatest asset in the successful prosecution of their mission. It would add at least an extra day to their trek, and that was too much time to sacrifice to the gods of caution.

"Sorry, Sergeant," he said after Minnevitch had spoken his piece. "But I won't circle the farm. Making a wide detour means marching through the forest and then across some rugged mountain country. It would add another day at least to our march. Pass the word for the men to stand alert, though," he concluded.

"Move out, men! Across that farm! Look alive!" the lieutenant shouted.

The Thunderbirds began filing out of the forest toward the farmstead two abreast. The scene was a familiar one to most of the men, who had themselves come from farm country.

All of them were struck by signs of the desolation that war had visited on this farm. The farmstead was in a state of complete dishevelment. It had gotten the stuffing smashed out of it by rounds from German 88s. Many of the dogfaces could not help thinking of their own rural backgrounds and transposing the scene they witnessed over the memories of home.

WITHIN THE dummy haystacks, the SS commandos waited with the patience of spiders for their prey to reach the center of the web. The Panzer tank also waited, just behind the stone frame of the gutted and abandoned farmhouse.

Through field glasses, Major Wolf Heilig watched the Americans come on. Closer, just a little closer, he thought to himself.

PRIVATE MATTHEW O'BANNON lit up a cigarette and handed the crumpled pack of Old Gold to his buddy. He was in the middle of a story about the strange things his girlfriend back home liked doing in bed.

In the middle of a sentence, Amboy suddenly got a funny look in his eyes. The look in Amboy's eyes was so funny that his buddy O'Bannon wanted to ask him what the hell was the matter.

At that moment the Nazi commander barked the order to commence the attack into the microphone of his radio. The order was instantly translated into action by his men. The signal sprang shut the jaws of the Nazi trap with the speed and deadliness of a rattler striking its prey.

The trapdoor front of one dummy haystack suddenly dropped down with a thud. Nazi soldiers were positioned behind the ugly black tripod of a Czech VZ37 medium machine-gun.

At the same time the muzzle of a tank turret smashed through the stone wall of the abandoned farmhouse shell. It was immediately followed by the glacis of the Panzer Mark IV. The tank rolled quickly, then stopped suddenly as the big cannon pivoted on its turret.

The clanking steel monstrosity juddered forward as its cannon muzzle swung in the direction of the American infantry column. Those soldiers at the rear of the column turned and tried to run back to the protection of the woods surrounding the farmstead perimeter, but yet more Panzers were now appearing from the woods, where they had been waiting in ambush to deal with stragglers.

The whole damned unit had walked straight into a German trap, Smilin' Mike Calhoun realized. And he had been the pied piper who had danced them right smack into it. And there wasn't a lovin' thing any of them could do about it now except hit the dirt, pass the ammunition and curse their goddamn awful luck.

**15**

"*Achtung! Achtung!*" blared the strident voice from the bullhorn mounted on the gun turret of the Panzer tank that had smashed its way out of the farmhouse.

"Escape is hopeless. You are completely surrounded! Surrender immediately and you will be treated fairly according to the rules set forth at the Geneva Convention. Refuse to obey and you will be shown no mercy."

Smilin' Mike Calhoun now wished he had listened to the advice Minnevitch had offered only a couple of minutes earlier. What a damned fool he had been. Spotters must have sighted the column hours ago and set up the ambush at a farm they knew the column had to cross.

The patrol team probably drove right into the trap and never stood a chance. And now it would be his men who would pay the price for his stupidity. Funny how quickly things could change in this war with deadly finality.

The captain could not forget that he had led his men straight to the slaughter like so many sheep. A broiling anger made his guts feel as though a steel ball were rolling around inside and made the sides of his jaw tighten in involuntary spasms.

Through field glasses from his position in the turret of the Panzer tank, SS Major Wolf Heilig scanned the perimeter of the farmstead.

Heilig satisfied himself that the American force was completely cut off from all escape routes. The Panzers and machine-gun crews had given them no options whatever.

The trap had been closed with the speed and precision of the blitzkrieg that characterized the German approach to victory in total war.

"We are waiting for your reply," the major barked over the public-address system when several more minutes had passed without an answer to his demands. "You have no choice but to surrender. You have precisely five minutes to make up your minds," he said finally, "after that we will commence firing. You have been warned."

In the strained silence that followed the major's warning, Minnevitch courted enemy fire as he sprinted and rolled toward the captain's position.

"You were right after all, Sergeant," Smilin' Mike told him bitterly. "Like they say, in hindsight even a fool is a genius. I wish I'd listened to you."

"Don't come down too hard on yourself, Cap'n," Minnevitch said to the embittered officer. "There was no way anybody could have known what those krauts were up to. I was going by blind instinct, and it turned out to be right. I could just as easily have been wrong, though."

"What really matters is what we do now," said Smilin' Mike. "We're completely cut off, that's apparent. How do you vote, Sergeant? Do you favor surrender?"

"I'd rather pry off my nuts with a rusty can opener first, sir," Minnevitch said without hesitation. "I'm sure I'm speaking for the men, too."

"Lieutenant, how do you vote?" Calhoun asked Canfield.

"The same as Minnevitch, sir," Canfield answered, clutching his rifle.

"I guess that decides the issue, gentlemen," Calhoun said, new life returning to his eyes and conviction to his voice. "Pass it on. Tell the men to open up on my signal. Every man is to try to escape in the confusion of the fighting. Those who make it will try to find their way back behind our own lines and report our position."

As the captain's orders were passed on through the ranks, Major Heilig was growing impatient. Consulting his wrist chronometer, he saw that the amnesty period he had given the Americans was fast drawing to a close.

"Your time is almost up," he shouted into the microphone in his hand. "For the last time, give—"

Heilig's words were lost in the din of the sudden gunfire coming from the Americans. For a moment the SS man was too stunned to realize what was happening.

He had never for a moment entertained the possibility that the Americans would choose to die rather than surrender. Apparently, though, precisely that was happening.

The major ducked inside and dogged down the hatch of the Panzer. "Fire on them, you idiot! *Mach schnell! Mach schnell!*" he bellowed at the top of his lungs, ordering his gunner to open up.

The Panzer roared as fire and smoke belched from the gun turret. The whistling of the speeding projectile cleaved the air as it zoomed through space on a terminal trajectory toward the hunkering Thunder-birds.

The shell struck with a thunderous *KAHHHH-BLAMMMM* that shook the ground, throwing up a curtain of smoke and earth. The shell crater was empty when the smoke cleared. Men sheltering within had been disintegrated by the high explosive.

Even as the Panzer fired, the camouflaged machine-gun crews opened up from their well-fortified positions. The chattering MG34s crisscrossed the battlefield with glowing tracers, and the chatter of blow-back-driven death filled the air.

The heavy-caliber machine-gun rounds mangled flesh and shattered bone as they struck their targets. The pointmen among the Oklahomans died jerking like marionettes as hot steel laid them to waste. Lieutenant Hank Canfield was among the first to catch a bullet. A moment before he died, he had glimpsed Private Buddy Kelso's face as Kelso ran past him, and suddenly realized that it had been Kelso who'd jumped him back in Naples.

As the Panzer rolled forward, its gun swiveled around, belching fire and steel like some hellish mechanical dragon, and its threads crushed men as though they were worms. With ponderous savagery, the Nazi war machine was on the move.

SERGEANT JOE MINNEVITCH turned from the bulging-eyed corpse of the dogface lying beside him and peered up from the rim of the shell crater where he and several other Thunderbirds had taken refuge from the death blitz of the Nazi counterattack.

In the confusion of battle he had lost his bearings. Firing back at the machine gunners who had pinned them down, Minnevitch hurled a grenade and blew the German fire pit to kingdom come in a bright flash of light and a storm of jagged shrapnel.

More Thunderbirds were now charging desperately through the dense, acrid smoke swathing the battle-field in a cordite-stinking shroud. German storm troopers were racing forward to stop them in their tracks. Their Schmeisser submachine guns chattered away, hurling and spitting flesh-eating parabellums at the Americans while the tommy guns of the GIs sang a grim counterpoint to the savage martial chorus.

His nostrils filled with the reek of gunpowder, his eyes hard and menacing, Minnevitch fired his Thompson SMG through the choking cordite clouds and took out two Nazi gunners who had targeted him for destruction.

Charging past the dead gunners, he ran like hell for the line of trees where the forest began at the edge of the battlefield. The death zone was choked with the black haze of high-explosive rounds and the even blacker smoke from burning German armor. The result was a fog of battle that concealed friend and foe alike until the combatants came face-to-face with one another.

Hidden by the black battle pall, Minnevitch hot-footed it toward the edge of the combat zone, bent on escape, convinced he was moving in the right direction by the diminishing sound of the battle and the gradual lifting of the fog as he progressed.

Suddenly a figure loomed up out of the fog almost directly in front of him. Minnevitch raised his tommy and tightened his finger on the trigger in case it was a German.

"Don't shoot, Sarge. It's me, Kelso," the figure shouted. Minnevitch felt something coiled tightly inside him relax as he lowered his weapon slightly. "What the hell's going on, Sarge?" Kelso asked as they both hustled into the forest beyond the battle zone.

"You said it for me," Minnevitch told the private. "Hell's going on. Let's make tracks."

Porting their weapons, their eyes peeled for Germans, the GI Joes dogtrotted into the woods. Behind them the sounds of battle were already beginning to die down. By then the battalion of Thunderbirds that had set out from Sainte-Maxime only days before were one of two things: casualties of war or prisoners of Hitler's Nazi Reich.

## 16

Minnevitch and Kelso trudged cautiously through the sparse woods encircling the farmstead. Movement through the trees suddenly caught Minnevitch's eye. Signaling to the other Thunderbird to take cover with gun at the ready by raising his thumb and sticking out his index finger, Minnevitch jumped behind a tree and waited.

Hefting their weapons, Minnevitch and Kelso waited, ready to jump the soldiers who they hoped were fellow stragglers taking flight from the ambush but who might just as easily be part of a German recon patrol. Luckily the strangers turned out to be Amboy, Haystacks, Mutt and four other Thunderbirds, privates Dunn, Fontana, Tinker and Sperling.

"Hey, over here!" Minnevitch called.

"Judas Priest!" Amboy exclaimed, recognizing the sergeant's voice, leaning back against a tree and shouldering an M-1 rifle. "I thought for a second you guys were krauts."

"The feeling was mutual," said Minnevitch gruffly. He looked around at the dogfaces fallen out here and there in the woods. "Anybody else make it out of that ambush?"

The dogfaces shook their heads. "Uh-uh," each of them said. It looked as though the ragged group of stragglers who succeeded in slipping away from the

Nazi net were all of the battalion that were left to carry on.

BY 1355 HOURS the small unit consisting of the escapees of the German ambush was out of the forest and back on the road. They were heading southeast in the general direction of Sainte-Maxime. When the road looped off to the north, they crossed the road and headed across an open field of low grass.

Their objective was to get back behind their own lines and report what had happened to the battalion. It was easier said than done, though. After the ambush, odds were that the woods would be crawling with German patrols. The chances of the lot of them making it back behind their own lines were not too damned good.

Suddenly death came swooping out of the sun, screaming like a great bird of prey.

It was the scream of the Stuka dive-bomber. The sound that once heard would never be mistaken for anything else was produced by the whine of the airstream over the Stuka's frame and by special drive sirens powered by the wind.

Hundreds of feet up, the pilot of the German *Sturzkampfbomber,* or dive-bomber, made visual contact with the Americans emerging into a clearing in which there were the ruins of a stone farmhouse. Driven by a powerful 1200 horsepower Junkers Jumo 211 engine, the plane climbed rapidly.

Reaching the ceiling of its flight envelope, the Stuka pilot immediately put the attack aircraft into a steep power dive. His finger flexed and tightened on the trigger of the two fixed 7.90 mm MG17 machine guns mounted on the Stuka's wings as the earth spun dizzyingly below him. He would use the guns soon, but not just yet.

As the Stuka's nose dipped earthward, the plane resembled nothing so much as a hawk swooping down on its prey. From the ground it would appear that the plane flew straight out of the sun.

It was a trick that the pilot had used before. Blinded by the sun, his intended targets would not even be able to see him until the plane was right on them. They could only hear the sound of the Stuka swooping down and run like frightened rats.

The Stuka's distinctive landing gear had been deliberately designed to resemble the talons of some enormous mechanical bird of prey. As the Stuka gained velocity on its downward sweep, the plane's wind-driven drive sirens gave out a scream that presaged the stuttering fire of its front-mounted machineguns.

*Wheeeerrrr!*

The embodiment in Krupp steel of the Nazi death eagle swooped down with the spine-chilling screech of damnation itself. Now the Stuka reached treetop level, and the pilot finally opened up with both his guns.

Twin lances of 7.90 mm bullets blazed across the open field. Slamming into the earth, their tremendous impact threw clods of earth and spinning chunks of shattered rock high into the air.

The Thunderbirds hustled toward the cover of a big irrigation ditch swollen by recent rains, hearing the scream of the metal beast as the Stuka overshot their position. Suddenly its wing-mounted machine guns fell silent, and there was only the receding roar of the Stuka's engines.

But only for a moment.

In that pulse beat of time, the Stuka pilot banked the plane steeply and wheeled round for another strafing run at the American targets, coming in so low that the plane's undercarriage seemed almost to skim the ground. The dogfaces could see the sun glint off its cockpit window and the Luftwaffe cross painted on the olive drab fuselage.

The German flyboy opened up at the instant he got his targets back in the range of his chatter guns. Instants later the MG17 machine guns were spitting out their rounds at a cycling rate of 850 rounds per minute.

Minnevitch flattened. The Stuka could drop either its main 550-pound bomb or its load of 110-pounders and blow them off the face of the earth. The Nazi pilot hadn't done so already because bullets were cheaper, and with ammo in short supply, he was saving the heavy ordnance for bigger game.

But once the pilot got tired of playing aerial cat-and-mouse, he'd drop part of his bomb load and cream their asses good.

"Amboy, gimme your rifle," Minnevitch shouted.

"How come, Sarge?"

"Because I wanna bake you a cake," he retorted. "Just make with the rifle."

Amboy handed Minnevitch the rifle as he watched the sergeant rummage through his field pack and bring out two M-17 rifle grenade rounds. The rounds were constructed of special adapters that screwed into the fuse cavity of a conventional Mk2A1 grenade body.

Fitted over the muzzle of a rifle, a gun could then be deployed as a grenade launcher with an operating range of over two hundred yards.

The sergeant's plan was to take the Stuka head-on. Risky, certainly. Suicidal, sure. But the Stuka would total them all if he couldn't get it first.

The pilot was good, and he demonstrated his aerial prowess behind the controls, making low passes that barely skirted the fields. His arrogance was his weak point, though. He was bringing the Stuka in so low on his strafing runs that with the right timing, maybe Minnevitch could hit it with one of the grenades.

As the Stuka roared overhead and spun around for another pass, the sergeant fitted one M-17 grenade launcher to Amboy's M-1, and attached the other rifle grenade to his own tommy, now set on semi-auto.

Because of the explosive power and range of the grenade, Minnevitch knew that in order to kayo the Stuka, he would not only need to score a direct hit in a vulnerable area, but also launch the round at the precise instant the Stuka was almost upon him.

An instant sooner or later, and they'd be deader than a cathouse waiting room on Christmas Eve. There would be no second chance to kill the Nazi sky eagle.

As the Stuka screamed overhead, the pilot expertly hugging the deck so that the dive-bomber's underbelly was no more than a dozen feet above the surface of the field, Minnevitch jumped from an irrigation ditch in which he had taken cover.

Inside the cockpit, the pilot scowled. He saw the American GI Joe leap up suddenly, defying him to kill him. How could he hope to survive the onslaught of his chattering machine guns? The Stuka pilot squeezed the trigger harder, shooting out hundreds of rounds of ammo per minute, confident of scoring a fast kill.

But still the American soldier stood his ground. Even as the twin lines of 7.90 mm machine-gun bullets tore up clods of earth inches from his body, the GI did not move. Miraculously the bullets didn't strike him. But the miracle would not continue for very much longer.

All the Stuka pilot needed to do was keep his finger on the trigger and careen the plane toward the American. He could now make out his features. When he did, he received a shock. The American was smiling, the butt of a cigar clenched between his teeth.

"Hey, kraut," Minnevitch said through gritted teeth as he squeezed the triggers of both rifles, "have a couple of live ones on me."

In twin puffs of smoke the M-17 rifle grenades blasted toward the onrushing Stuka. Time stood still in an eternity that was compressed into a single moment. Then, suddenly there was impact as Minnevitch hit the dirt.

One grenade round, then the other, blew with twin white flashes. At once, black smoke streamed in thick clouds from just forward of the Stuka's wings. The terrifying scream of the attack plane was beginning to splutter and die. Within the cockpit the German pilot scowled as panic gripped him.

Desperately he tried to put the Stuka's nose back up, but the dive-bomber had been hit at the lowest angle of its trajectory. The plane was steadily and rapidly losing altitude and there wasn't anything he could do to change that fact.

Although the pilot pulled back on the stick as hard as he could, the plane still would not respond.

The Stuka pilot didn't even have time to scream as the dive-bomber struck the side of a hill and exploded into a yellow-black ball of fire. The pilot was incinerated instantly, his body blackened to a crisp as the wreckage disintegrated, while behind him, the Stuka's tail-gunner burned like a scarecrow struck by summer lightning.

"Gee, Sarge," Amboy asked Minnevitch, "where'd you learn to shoot like that?"

"In a penny arcade, wisenheimer," Minnevitch returned. Then the sergeant rose up from the ground and dusted the leaf litter and earth from his fatigues.

"Kelso, check the wreckage for survivors," he barked when the world stopped spinning.

"Right, Sarge."

Kelso moved out and got as close as he could to the main part of the burning wreck of the downed Stuka. Fragments of the once-sleek frame had been scattered all over the place by the tremendous force of the explosion. There was no sign of either member of the two-man crew. Satisfied that nothing could have survived the crash, Kelso dogtrotted back to Minnevitch.

"Nix on the krauts, Sarge," he reported, shaking his head. "Old Max and Fritz are kaput."

"Okay."

Minnevitch realized that he was bathed in sweat from head to foot. That had been a damned close one by any yardstick.

He squinted toward the site of the explosion as he fished in the top pockets of his field jacket for his last couple of Phillies and jammed one of the stogies into his mouth. When those were gone, there wouldn't be any more left, but it was even money as to whether he'd last longer than the smokes or vice versa.

Did the German flyboy have a chance to radio back their position? Minnevitch wondered silently, but he figured that even if he hadn't, the crash of the Stuka could have easily been noticed from German observation posts sited in the hills. At that very moment there might well be dozens of observers radioing the position of the crash to local troop garrisons.

"Move out, you lovin' heroes," Minnevitch told his ragtag unit. "Move out fast and don't look behind you. That Stuka crew might have put every German from here to Berlin on our keisters."

## 17

The forest was eerily silent, no different than a grave-yard at midnight. The column of doughfoots walked through it, holding their breath like superstitious old women in the presence of invisible evil, scanning the treetops for concealed snipers and scouring the road for signs of German ambushers.

Their nerves were on edge. But that was under-standable. So were their lives.

Amboy thought he could hear the blood pumping through his own veins. Mutt wasn't even thinking about Rita Hayworth anymore. Haystacks was star-ing straight ahead with eyes that burned like circles of hot cigarette ash, thinking about how it might feel to catch a bullet and about the different places where he might catch one. Minnevitch had Fontana on his mind. The dogface looked ready to crack, and Min-nevitch wondered when it would happen and how.

If he'd ever seen a case of battle fatigue in the mak-ing, it was Fontana. The soldier was saucer eyed with fear. During a rest break he'd thrown himself down on the ground and wept into the dirt. A man in his con-dition could wind up getting everybody in the detail wiped out without half trying.

The GIs had been taking it on the arches for what seemed like days, even years, but it had really been only a few hours since their brush with the Stuka. Each new stretch of woods looked the same as the others they had passed through. About the only breaks in the maddening monotony were the enemy spotter planes that occasionally droned overhead.

This confirmed Minnevitch's hunch that the Stuka pilot had either radioed their positions back to base just before the crash or that the Germans had somehow gotten wise to the fact that not all the GIs caught in the trap at the farmstead had been captured in the ambush.

"Sarge, I hear something," Kelso sang out. He put his ear to the ground and listened carefully. "Sounds a hell of a lot like heavy armor. You don't think it's the U.S.O. do ya, Sarge?"

"I think it's Fred Astaire and Ginger Rogers, Kelso," Minnevitch shot back, "but what the fuck do I know."

"Moving in our direction, Sarge," Kelso said, still with his ear to the ground.

Now Minnevitch thought he heard the sound, too. It was the telltale rumble of a patrol. A German patrol, it went without saying, and probably hunting for their hides in all likelihood. The cheeks of his butt clenched, and he could feel the sweat break out on his face. Here came the shit all over again, and the proverbial fan blades were spinning like crazy. When it finally hit, look out!

"Kelso, go climb a tree and see what you can scout out," Minnevitch barked. "Here, take these binoculars with you."

He tossed his field glasses at Kelso, who hustled to carry out the sergeant's orders, shimmying up a big elm with the ease of a circus acrobat.

Minnevitch reconned the road and the forest flanking it for a few minutes. "Amboy and Mutt, you mothers shag it over there behind those two boulders on one side of the road, see 'em? The rest of you goldbricks take cover in the ditch on the right of the road. Hop to it, doughfoots."

Minnevitch stressed only the right side because he didn't want his own men firing at each other from either side of the road. He'd lost enough to the enemy and didn't want to lose any more to his own guys.

Up in the branches of the big elm tree, Kelso put the eyepieces of the field glasses to his face and focused down on the road. Now he clearly saw that it was a mechanized German column rolling toward the squad on the narrow, winding mountain road.

The first things that caught Kelso's eye were the two motorcyclists who rode at the head of the column. They came suddenly out of the shadows at a bend in the road into a patch of sunlight. Each motorcycle was equipped with a sidecar in which a Schmeisser-armed Waffen SS outrider sat and scanned the forest to either side of the road.

Behind the cyclists there came an armored patrol car. It was a half-track with two front-mounted heavy machine guns jutting forward like the antennae of some gigantic armored beetle.

Following the half-track was a personnel carrier. About twenty storm troopers were sitting ten to a row and facing one another behind the cab. Towed behind the personnel carrier was a small field piece.

From the insignia on the field gray greatcoats worn by the Nazis, Kelso could see that they were Waffen SS storm troopers. He sucked in his breath. A breed of

Aryan "superman" not to be trifled with by any estimation.

Nazis, not just Germans. It was a distinction that GIs in Europe had learned the hard way. A true Nazi was ten times the trouble of an ordinary Wehrmacht soldier.

Soon Minnevitch heard an owl hoot from the trees overhead. Only it wasn't an owl. It was Buddy Kelso signaling confirmation that an enemy patrol was heading down the road.

"Whatcha got for me?" Minnevitch asked Kelso when he'd climbed down from his arboreal vantage point shortly thereafter.

"The picture don't look too pretty, Sarge," Kelso said. He related what he'd seen to Minnevitch, adding that the column was about a mile down the road and moving fast.

Minnevitch sized up the situation right away. There were only a couple of minutes to get ready to take on the patrol.

He and his band of stragglers could try to make a run for it, but maybe the Germans were carrying some information that would be useful to their side. They had been outfoxed one time too many, he decided.

Minnevitch issued his orders quickly. "Get your heads down," he said. "Look alive, you heroes, we're in a tight spot. Open up on the column when the cyclists reach that boulder up ahead there. Then start the shit flying. Take out the armored car first if you can, then go for the transport. We're outnumbered about ten to one, so our only chance is to hit the krauts before they know what's happening."

The entire unit readied its weapons. The patrol appeared suddenly around a bend in the narrow forest road minutes later, faster than any dogface had expected.

When the point of the column reached the boulder, the Thunderbirds opened up full blast, showering the patrol column with lead. Minnevitch hurled grenades at the leading half-track and hosed it down with .45-caliber autofire from his tommy gun. The scout vehicle picked up speed to escape the trap, but it began to weave precariously, zigzagging from one side of the road to the other.

Moments later it lost traction completely and skidded off the surface of the road. A barrage of firing finished off anything inside it.

The rest of the unit opened up on the Nazi soldiers in the personnel carrier. Schmeisser fire answered their volley, but the dogfaces pitched the hand grenades that hung ready on chest webbing, and soon the German guns sputtered to silence, those who wielded them hanging limply over the sides of the vehicle.

It was all over for the Germans before they could orient themselves. They had not been expecting the surprise attack and they had paid for their lack of vigilance with their lives.

"Sarge, over here!"

Minnevitch saw to his astonishment that the doors of the kayoed half-track had opened, and two Germans were staggering out, coughing in the acrid smoke that poured from it.

Minnevitch pointed his gun at the Germans. *"Raus! Raus!"* he shouted. "Come out of there and *machen sie schnell* about it,'' he yelled at them. They obeyed the American sullenly.

One of them was an officer, a major from the insignia on his uniform. The other survivor was a lieutenant. As he emerged, the major pulled a Mauser machine pistol holstered at his Sam Browne belt and got off a couple of shots. The GIs automatically returned fire, but as they did, the major suddenly grabbed the lieutenant and held him in front of his body as a human shield.

As the riddled corpse of the lieutenant slumped to the muddy forest floor, spewing out his life blood, the major tried to make a break for it, throwing down his now-empty Mauser. But Minnevitch didn't want to let this one get away.

The German was a big fish and worth more to them alive than dead. From a flat-out run, he launched himself after the fleeing officer in a flying tackle and brought him down in a thrashing heap.

It was over in just a couple of minutes. Minnevitch pulled the Hun to his feet and searched him for concealed weapons but found none.

*"Sprechen sie Englisch?"* Minnevitch asked as he marched his captive back toward the rest of the unit.

The officer responded to his question in German. Minnevitch didn't understand what he was saying, but he got the drift that the German wasn't too impressed by what had happened to his troops.

"Sperling, front and center," Minnevitch sang out. "You speak German, right? Well, translate for me."

Minnevitch turned to Amboy and instructed him to search the dead bodies for anything that looked important but not to grab any souvenirs. If they were captured by the enemy while carrying any personal effects belonging to dead Germans, they would likely be executed on the spot.

"Hey, Sarge—something's burning inside the half-track!" Minnevitch suddenly heard Dunn call out.

"Go see what it is. Hurry up," Minnevitch shouted as Dunn scrambled into the half-track. He came out minutes later, carrying a smoldering military pouch that he flung to the ground and stomped on to put out the fire.

"Here, Sarge," Dunn said, handing the pouch to Minnevitch. As the sergeant opened the charred canvas pouch and looked inside, the major suddenly lunged for it. Minnevitch clocked him across the side of his face with the butt of his Thompson, knocking him senseless to the forest floor.

"What the hell was that all about?" Dunn asked as he looked down at the major.

"I think I know," Minnevitch said, taking out the folded papers that were inside the canvas pouch. Unfolding them, he could see they were military maps of the area through which they were marching. The maps were stenciled in German with writing Minnevitch figured meant something like Top Secret.

When the German regained his senses, a couple of minutes' interrogation established that the patrol was in fact on the lookout for American GIs. But what was more important were the papers that the German was carrying on him.

While the sergeant was powwowing with the major, Tinker and Haystacks went through the pockets of the dead Germans from the personnel carrier. Attracted by the scent of fresh blood, blue-flies were already buzzing around the corpses. Before long the corpses would begin to stink like hell.

Their search didn't turn up anything important looking, and nothing of particular interest except for a photo that Tinker had slid from a wallet.

"Hot damn, what a knockout," Tinker exclaimed as he gazed appreciatively at the buxom fräulein shown in the picture. "Wouldn't mind a roll in the hay with a swell jane like her."

Neither Tinker nor Haystacks realized that one of the Germans lying near the road was only playing dead. As Tinker went on rifling the pocket of the soldier he'd taken the wallet from, hoping, despite the sergeant's orders, to find a good souvenir, the German suddenly sat up, pulled a long bayonet knife and plunged it to the hilt in Tinker's throat.

Tinker screamed in mortal agony and dropped the pictures of the blonde with the big bosom to try to pull out the dagger. Haystacks was firing his M-1 rifle into the German, firing into his head until there was nothing left but a ragged stump through which blood oozed darkly onto the leaf-littered earth.

Sagging to the ground, Tinker stared up at his buddy with glazing eyes. Now he saw a half dozen Haystackses, all melting into and out of one another, spinning around and around like distorted faces in a kaleidoscope.

"Hey, you're . . . you're . . ." Haystacks heard Tinker mutter as he stooped over him. Then Tinker shivered all over and finally went limp.

Later, when Tinker was in the ground, Minnevitch went back to interrogating the major. He was a tight-lipped son of a bitch, but the documents in the charred map case retrieved from the armored car told a lot more than he was willing to reveal. Something big was going on—something that headquarters back at Sainte-Maxime would damned well want to know.

CAPTAIN MIKE CALHOUN and the prisoners taken from TF 179 were being marched in a long column through a land made fallow by war. The only certainty about their future appeared to be that it would be spent as permanent guests of Hitler's so-called Thousand Year Reich.

The column of GI prisoners was marching steadily northward, deeper into occupied France and eventually Germany. The captain only knew what he had been told by the German officer who was in charge of the prisoners.

According to the officer, they were being marched to a POW camp deeper in occupied France, from where they were to be sent to Germany along with the withdrawing Nazi troops. There was nothing more to find out, except that the future looked damned bleak. The war was over for Smilin' Mike and his men, the German officer had added. The prisoners might as well accept their fate and do as they were ordered.

To make sure that they obeyed, the Germans kept their guns well trained on the prisoners at all times. Smilin' Mike knew there was no hope of escape. Their mission had been a failure. Worst of all, he was the one to take the blame.

**18**

The Nazi patrol was again mobile, roaring and clanking through the wooded French hill country. It had changed in two important respects, though. Instead of Germans, its personnel were Americans, and there was only one motorcycle escort instead of the original two.

His face hidden behind goggles, Kelso drove the cycle in the uniform of a Wehrmacht enlisted man attached to the German motor battalion. Mutt rode in the sidecar. He toted the Schmeisser SMG of the man who had originally occupied his place and now was at rest in a shallow grave in the picturesque French countryside.

Inside the cab of the armored half-track behind the sidecar were Minnevitch, Fontana and the captured Nazi, SS Sturmbannführer Rudolf Bannekker. Neither Minnevitch nor Fontana had put on the uniforms of the dead Germans, but still wore their GI-issue fatigues. Minnevitch kept his eyes trained on both the prisoner and Fontana to make sure Fontana didn't crack.

Amboy and Dunn occupied the passenger area of the personnel carrier that trundled along right behind the armored car. Both of the GIs wore captured German greatcoats and ported Wehrmacht-issue Gewehr-43 rifles and Schmeisser MP-40 SMGs taken off the terminated Nazi troopers.

In the cab sat Privates Sperling and Haystacks, the GI dogfaces also wearing captured German uniforms. They had spent the better part of an hour stripping corpses and picking out the uniforms that fitted them best and showed the least damage.

The next order of business involved burying the former owners of the uniforms in a shallow mass grave in the forest where, if undiscovered for another month or so, they would hopefully remain hidden until at least the following spring.

After that, the captured German vehicles had to be put back into some semblance of working order, though there wasn't much they could do about the telltale scorch marks from grenade strikes or pockmarks from automatic fire.

Minnevitch had glimpsed the possibility of atoning for the crushing defeat the Thunderbird patrol had suffered at German hands by dealing them a deal as dirty as the one they'd dealt the Thunderbirds.

The documents they had discovered in the map case that the German major had tried to set on fire made mention of some kind of massive engineering installation to the north.

What in blazes the Germans were doing by engaging in a major construction project even as their troops were withdrawing from the area was a big mystery. A mystery that Minnevitch was determined to solve.

UNKNOWN TO THE Americans, hostile eyes were watching the armored column as it threaded its way up the narrow mountain road. Marcel Dupré, known to the Allies by his code name "Voltaire," and his band of French Maquis had eyeballed the German column only minutes before.

To smash the armored patrol of the hated occupiers would be a victory worth risking much for. Therefore, Marcel had ordered Émile and Philippe, his two trusted lieutenants, and the rest of his men to ambush the German column.

Dupré assigned himself the task of keeping the driver of the motorcycle in the sights of the German Panzerfaust rocket launcher that he had captured from the hated enemy during a previous action.

Now Marcel had the Panzerfaust trained on the armored car's tracks, a spot he knew from past experience to be the vehicle's most vulnerable point. Take out the lead vehicle, and killing the rest of the Nazis would be easily accomplished. So regimented was the German soldier that he was virtually incapable of acting or thinking on his own accord. Fit only to obey orders, the enlisted men would be easy targets once their leaders were dealt with.

But inside the cab of the armored half-track, Minnevitch had spotted movement among the trees. His first impression was that more of the enemy were waiting in the ambush, but that didn't add up right. Why would they want to waylay their own armor? Besides, the figure he'd glimpsed was not in German field gray nor in the camouflage fatigues of certain SS elite units.

Putting two and two together brought Minnevitch to the conclusion that partisans and not Germans were positioned just ahead of them on the road, French partisans. If that were the case, then they were certainly setting up a kill trap, mistaking them for Nazis.

Quickly stopping the rig so fast that Haystacks in the cab of the transport behind crashed into his rear, the sergeant jumped through the hatch with his hands raised, wondering what the fuck to say. Whatever it was, he knew that he had to spit it out in two seconds flat, or he'd probably wind up catching a bullet.

*"Maurice Chevalier!"* he finally settled on, hollering it at the top of his lungs.

Marcel was preparing to trigger the Panzerfaust rocket, but now he was too startled to fire. What he saw was a soldier in the khaki combat fatigues of an American GI, standing with hands raised from the top of the armored half-track and shouting the name of France's greatest leading man like a madman. Marcel glanced at Émile, who shrugged in reply, as if to say that war certainly was a crazy thing.

Minnevitch didn't speak French, but he hoped that the Frenchmen would be able to understand what he was caterwauling at the top of his lungs. Luckily the name of the greatest French lover of the century was the last thing any German would shout, and that fact alone prompted Marcel to order his men to hold their fire until he could establish what on earth was going on.

Soon the Americans were climbing out of the captured vehicles, and Minnevitch began to explain to Marcel and the rest of the guerrillas just what had happened to the column.

"You have netted yourself quite a big fish," Marcel explained as he caught sight of the German major. "This one is a stinking pig. He is well-known throughout these hills. He is a butcher who has sent many innocent women and children to the concentration camps. We should execute such a dog as he on the spot."

"Nix to that, brother," Minnevitch returned. "Kill the kraut, and you take away our pass into that secret installation up the road a ways."

"You are crazy, American," Marcel said to the sergeant. "You cannot hope to masquerade as a Bosch officer and get away with it. This Nazi swine would give you away, even if it meant his own death, as well."

"That's a chance I'm prepared to take," Minnevitch told Marcel. He understood full well that they were in the Maquis's territory and in order to succeed he would need their goodwill and help.

"After we're through, you can put the kraut in a big kettle and boil him in oil, for all I care," he went on, "but right now I'm asking you to play ball with us."

Marcel and his second in command conferred in rapid French, punctuating their palaver with the most complicated hand gestures Minnevitch had seen since he'd left Naples.

Finally Marcel told the American that they would be permitted to go their way. However, since the Americans were obviously not in their right minds, Marcel and his partisan band would tag along and keep watch when the Americans ventured into the vicinity of the German installation. These GIs might be fools, thought Marcel, but after all, they did happen to be fighting on the same side.

NIGHT HAD ALREADY FALLEN when two German officers and a sergeant arrived at the main gate of the high-security installation. Big klieg lights were mounted on twenty-foot-high masts to illuminate the work zone so the construction details could labor around the clock. Regardless of the late hour, construction activity was taking place everywhere at a feverish pace.

With Sperling as their spokesman, Minnevitch and the German, Major Bannekker, went into the base, informing the guards that they were on a surprise inspection tour. The strategy worked, and they were directed to the commandant's bunker. Conditioned not to question authority—especially when orders were delivered at the top of an officer's lungs—the German soldier was immediately cowed by the trio in impressive Waffen SS uniforms.

With the pistol in the pocket of Minnevitch's Nazi greatcoat only an inch or two from his back, Major Bannekker behaved himself, not doubting for a second that Minnevitch would risk his own death by shooting him if he made a false move.

The American was not to be trifled with—the major had seen that much from the first. For the present, at least, he would be forced to play along with the GI's wishes.

The trio was received by the installation's commander, Colonel Hasso Kreuger. Since Kreuger did not appear too surprised to see them, Minnevitch suspected that the soldier in the guardhouse had phoned the base CO to give advance warning of the "surprise" inspection.

Kreuger didn't seem to mind the uninvited guests, however, and in fact seemed quite pleased. He shook their hands and launched into a string of rapid-fire German aimed at Minnevitch, who did not understand a word of it. A few tense seconds passed as Colonel Kreuger stared at Minnevitch, obviously expecting some sort of a reply.

Minnevitch was rescued by Sperling, who spoke up in his place, exchanging a few words in rapid German with Kreuger. Instantly the colonel's expression changed completely, and he clapped Minnevitch on the shoulder, concluding with a few more words in German. Then he turned and gestured for the group to follow him.

"What in the name of Mary and Joseph was that all about?" Minnevitch asked Sperling as soon as he was able to speak to him unheard.

"Actually it's kinda funny, Sarge," Sperling returned in a whisper from the side of his mouth. "What the kraut colonel was saying was how your face and physique were the picture of the perfect Aryan specimen. He said that if Hitler had a few thousand men like you, Germany would win the war in two weeks."

"So how did you put him off?"

"I told him you couldn't answer because you had lost your voice. When the colonel clapped you on the shoulder he was telling you to get some good American sour-mash whiskey and drink it, claiming it cured everything. He said he'd like to offer you some, but all he had was schnapps."

The rest of the visit to the base passed without incident. Colonel Kreuger seemed only too happy to give them the Cook's tour of the installation. Kreuger pointed out with pride the fortifications under construction, following plans drawn up by no less a personage than Albert Speer himself.

In a way, Minnevitch couldn't blame the colonel for feeling proud of the achievement. The base was a truly impressive piece of construction work. Minnevitch was no expert, but it was apparent that the Germans weren't just whistling Dixie here.

Any way you cut it, the installation was major-league stuff. What they were building in the area was nothing less than a barrier of fortified pillboxes that were a smaller version of the Siegfried line in Germany.

From such fortified emplacements, the Nazis could hold off the invading Allied armies indefinitely. Nestled within the natural protection offered by the mountains, the Germans could prevent the Allied armies from linking up with their own forces in the north.

The ploy was ingenious. With the underground bunkers, the Germans could hold out against even the heaviest bombing missions that the Air Force could throw at them. Minnevitch realized that the most the Germans could really hope to accomplish was to hold off the Allied advance until the fall, but he figured that a holding action was what they wanted to begin with.

In Italy the Allies had allowed the Germans to dig in deep in the Aurunci Mountains. The German Winter line, as the fortifications had come to be known, had cost the Allies an entire season of bloody campaigning to reach the Liri Valley and the city of Rome.

Only with the spring had Ike's forces succeeded in penetrating the German defensive line, and by then Hitler had already pulled most of his troops out of Rome entirely, redirecting them to France, Belgium and the Russian front.

If Hitler were allowed to accomplish the same feat here in France, tens of thousands of battle-hardened Nazi troops could be deployed to beef up the thinly spread lines along the Saar and the Rhine rivers, which would become the final defensive bastion of the Nazi Reich. Such a tactic might well buy Hitler enough time to muster his forces for yet another assault.

By the end of the tour, Minnevitch had gotten himself an eyeful. Declining an offer to join Kreuger for a glass or two of good schnapps in his quarters as a substitute treatment for Minnevitch's laryngitis, the trio left the construction site through the main gate, just as they had entered it. A few hundred yards down the road, Minnevitch linked up with his own men and Marcel's underground fighters.

"You have the luck of the mad," Marcel told Minnevitch as he led them through the darkened forest. "I must confess that I never expected to see you alive again."

"I also have the face of a true Aryan," Minnevitch told Marcel with a wicked grin. "With the krauts that's always a big plus."

## 19

A natural limestone cavern located not far from the site of the Nazi installation served as the headquarters of Marcel Dupré and his band of French resistance fighters. Prehistoric hunters had used the cave millenia before. Their images of bison, giant sloth and woolly mammoth covered the rock walls.

The French freedom fighters and the Americans sat around a fire eating a Spartan meal of smoked sausage and hot tea supplemented with GI field rations. Big candles propped on the tops of captured Nazi helmets lit the cave in a flickering light.

The cans of chipped beef, ham, franks and beans were heated over tins of canned heat. To men used to the privations of battle and hungry enough to swallow dirt, the chow tasted better than the most expensive caviar.

The Americans and the Frenchmen swapped war stories as they sat around eating their grub. Most of the Frenchmen in Marcel's band were originally from Paris, but they had been drawn from all walks of life. Their backgrounds were diverse. One had been a doctor, another a schoolteacher, a third a painter, a fourth a shopkeeper and so on.

They shared a single common denominator, though: the lives they had led had been destroyed by the Germans. Each was now driven by a single goal: to kick the hated Germans out of *La Belle France* and make their beloved country free of the Nazi evil for all time.

After the meal was over, the group determined to get some rest, posting one of the Frenchmen as a lookout. Major Bannekker was tied up in a corner, and Pascal, one of the Maquis, was set to keep watch on him. Pascal had more on his mind than merely watching the German, though. As the other men inside the cave drifted off to exhausted slumber, Pascal cleaned his fingernails with the razor-sharp tip of his stiletto and eyed the major with glittering black eyes.

"For you, Bosch pig, I have something special," he whispered. "I deal with you right now. You kill my brother, Marat. I will avenge him right now. Soon you beg me to let you die. Now come, *allez!*"

Warning the German to keep silent or he would cut his throat immediately, Pascal led Bannekker outside at gunpoint.

"Here, Bosch, take this," he told the German when they had gone a few dozen feet into the forest, and flung a shovel at his feet. "It is with this that you will dig your own grave. You remember how, no? You should, for it is the same way you made Marat and hundreds of others prepare to meet their ends."

Pascal watched the German dig, anticipating with homicidal relish the moment when he would shoot him in the back of the head. That was what the Germans had done to Marat when they marched the occupants of their small village out into the countryside and began mass executions.

The reason that Nazis had committed such an atrocity was that the villagers had refused to give up Marcel and his partisans. For that crime they were killed in what the German military record termed a "just and legitimate retribution."

None had been spared. Small children were shot along with adults, and the life of an entire village was crushed out with unrelenting brutality.

Before him now was the obscene pig who had ordered the destruction of the village. Pascal did not give a damn about what happened to him or what the Americans needed Bannekker for. He knew only that his soul cried out for vengeance, and he was driven by the need to extract his vengeance now.

But Pascal's own lust for the German's blood had made him careless. It had taken his concentration from the Nazi for one critical instant. Quick to take advantage, Bannekker shoveled up a clod of French earth, but instead of throwing it onto the growing pile, he wielded the shovel in a vicious two-handed swipe that struck Pascal's gun hand, knocking the pistol to the ground.

"I should kill you now, you stinking French cockroach," Bannekker said through clenched teeth as with catlike quickness he recovered Pascal's dropped pistol. "But I need you. Now, get up and do as I tell you. *Mach schnell!*"

With Pascal walking ahead of him at gunpoint, Bannekker made his way toward the cave. He was determined to kill the Frenchmen and the American GIs rather than steal away like a thief in the night. Surprise was on his side, and he thought it would be possible to carry out this grim task before making his own escape.

Besides, Bannekker had a personal score to settle with the Americans. He was not about to let the ragtag collection of Americans and Frenchmen make a fool of him. His honor as an officer of the Reich and the Waffen SS demanded this.

As Bannekker and Pascal reached the cave mouth, they were challenged by Claude on sentry patrol.

"Halt!" Claude shouted, suddenly seeing figures appear through the dark curtain of trees.

At that moment Pascal spun around, grabbed the wrist of Bannekker's gun hand and wrestled for the pistol held by the German.

Claude kept the German covered with his carbine as the men grappled for possession of the gun, but at the last moment Bannekker turned. Claude's rifle had barked once, and Pascal caught the bullet intended for Bannekker in the small of his back. Before Claude could get off another round, the German shot him through the heart and turned to run back into the woods.

Hearing the sound of gunfire, Minnevitch was up in seconds. He reached the cave mouth in time to see Bannekker race into the forest. He didn't know what was happening, but understood that the Nazi was getting away. He didn't need to know any more. Minnevitch sprinted after the fleeing Nazi, then flattened himself against a tree as Bannekker snapped off a burst over his shoulder and made a beeline into the woods.

Minnevitch sped after him, determined to stop the prisoner and not bothered by being unarmed. In these woods, the sound of a gunshot carried like rolling thunder.

It was even money that the Germans in the area of these hills were on the alert for the slightest sound. The sound of a firefight would bring them out in force. Soon the enemy would be swarming over their position like hounds scenting the presence of a fox. If Bannekker were to be stopped, it needed to be done silently and swiftly, or it might well be curtains for them all.

Minnevitch caught up with Bannekker a few hundred yards into the woods. Bannekker aimed the pistol and pulled the trigger, but the hammer fell with a click on an empty chamber. He had used up all the bullets in the gun. With a curse on his lips, the German flung the useless weapon at Minnevitch to make a break for it while Minnevitch was forced to duck.

Swiftly recovering his balance, Minnevitch chased after the fleeing man and launched a flying tackle at his feet. They fell to the ground in a tangled heap of flailing arms and legs.

As they wrestled on the ground, the Nazi managed to roll on top. Pinning Minnevitch's arms with his knees, he balled his fists together and struck the American repeatedly across the jaw, making a sound like apples thrown against a wall.

Dazed, Minnevitch looked up as the Nazi grabbed a jagged rock and, grasping it tightly in both hands, raised it over his head. With a grunt he smashed it down at the American, who managed to jerk his head away at the last instant.

Blood spurted from Minnevitch's face as the cutting edge of the stone bit into his cheek. Before the stone could descend again to cave in his skull, the American summoned his last remaining ounce of strength and heaved the Nazi off.

Bannekker sprawled backward, the sharp stone flying from his hands. Minnevitch staggered to his feet, breathing hard. The world was spinning around like the walls of a carnival fun house. Bannekker had three heads and they were all spinning, too.

Bannekker launched a vicious kick that would have shattered the hip bone, had it connected. Dodging quickly aside, Minnevitch grabbed hold of the Nazi's boot and twisted hard. Giving a savage wrench, Minnevitch sent the man toppling like a felled oak, but he recovered his footing with the quickness of a cat, throwing dirt and dry leaves into Minnevitch's face.

Temporarily blinded, Minnevitch caught a sucker punch to the jaw that rocked him back on his heels. Then Bannekker lunged again, but Minnevitch was ready to sidestep the blow and follow through with a balled fist to Bannekker's jaw.

While Bannekker reeled about dazedly, Minnevitch quickly got behind him and clamped his head in a stranglehold. Realizing what was about to happen, Bannekker squirmed with all his might, but he had no more strength left to struggle.

Still seeing stars himself, Minnevitch continued applying pressure until he heard a sickening snap. Spluttering and gagging, the Nazi soon went limp in his hands.

Bannekker sagged to the earth and lay still, leaking blood from his nose and his mouth. Minnevitch wiped his own blood-streaked face and the large ugly gash on his right cheek with the back of his hand and started to trudge back to camp.

He took no more than two short steps. The next thing he knew, one of Marcel's men was beside him and applying a packet of sulfa powder to his injured cheek and bandaging the wound.

"Good work, my friend," Marcel told Minnevitch, and clapped him on the shoulder.

"Yeah," Minnevitch replied. "He was a tough son of a gun."

# BOOK FOUR:
# REAR-GUARD ACTION

Occupied France,
August 1944

**20**

*Sector Charlie-Easy*

Stalag 20 was comprised of dozens of long wooden barracks painted a military olive drab and surrounded by a double row of twenty-foot-high hurricane fencing. The prisoner-of-war camp was patrolled by German guards accompanied by Doberman pinschers on leather leads.

This particular German POW camp offered somewhat better accommodations than most others because it had been initially constructed as a base for German troops. With the rapid advances made by the Allies, though, the barracks buildings afforded a ready-made internment camp for Allied prisoners.

Among the approximately two thousand prisoners cooped up in Stalag 20, there were American, British and some Canadian prisoners. Most of them were American GIs, though, and the recent capture of hundreds of men in the ambush of TF 179 swelled the ranks of the prison camp by roughly a quarter of its occupancy level.

Captain Smilin' Mike Calhoun had led the survivors of the ambushed infantry battalion in a torturous march over rugged mountain country for many miles. Only brief rest stops had been allowed. The Germans were in no mood to be charitable to the captured GIs. They were losing ground everywhere in

France and had no love lost for those very same troops who were slaughtering them in droves.

Forced to move along relentlessly without food or water except what was occasionally offered by farmers and villagers in the countryside on their way to Stalag 20, the prisoners had a tough time of it. Many were beaten by their Nazi overseers and were stripped of their boots to make them tread barefoot over the rocky ground.

Some days later Smilin' Mike Calhoun and the other ranking soldiers were brought to the officers' barracks and introduced to the camp's senior officer, Colonel Colin Haversham of the British Expeditionary Forces. He had been captured with a company of British paratroops in the marshes beyond the beachheads of Normandy during the June invasion.

"Heard all about how Jerry got you chaps," Haversham began after shaking Calhoun's hand and motioning him to sit. There were only a few pieces of rickety-looking furniture in the barren room that served as his office. "Bad bit of business, that. However," Haversham continued as he sat down, "you'll be pleased to learn that we have succeeded in getting fair treatment from the Germans."

"Begging your pardon, sir," Calhoun said, "but how long do you think that will continue? I mean, the krauts are getting their asses kicked from here to Paris. By the way... can we speak freely here?"

Haversham motioned with his cane toward the flyspecked window, through which Calhoun could see a group of British prisoners hoeing a small garden. "If Jerry shows his bloody face, my chaps out there will tap on the window. We very thoroughly check for concealed microphones, as well. I can assure you we've more privacy here than when the Queen Mother goes for her morning, ah, constitutional.

"Now, as for your other question..." Haversham went on in the same dry manner. "I didn't want to break the news to you just yet, old man, but we've just received word that bloody Jerry intends to pack us off to Berlin within a fortnight."

"That's why our escape committee has been working overtime," put in the other officer, an American major named Wynn Robnett, who stood with his arms crossed. "The Brits here have been tunneling under the camp for months. Your men will be very helpful in the escape bid."

Calhoun's briefing continued, and when it was done, Calhoun was shown his bunk in the officers' barracks. He could see at a glance that strict military discipline was maintained at Stalag 20. The barracks were spotless, without a single sign of disorder. The men were well shaven and wearing clean if threadbare uniforms. They also appeared to be reasonably well fed.

Smilin' Mike had the clear impression that if anyone could pull off a mass escape from under the noses of the Germans, it would be Haversham and his men. Nevertheless, Calhoun wanted to know more details of the escape plans before he gave his full approval.

Although he was outranked by both Haversham and Robnett, Calhoun still felt his loyalty to his Oklahoma guardsmen transcended what the rule book said. But he needed to rejuvenate his mind and body, and soon he fell into an exhausted slumber on the hard barracks bunk.

*Sector Able-Bravo*

APPROXIMATELY a hundred miles to the north of Stalag 20, work on the secret line of pillboxes connected by a network of underground bunkers was progressing at a rapid pace.

Colonel Hasso Kreuger had spared no pains to ensure that everything was in order as he welcomed a most important guest from Berlin. The guest was none other than Albert Speer, the personal architect of Adolf Hitler.

Positioning themselves on a high scaffold, which afforded a view of the entire construction site, Kreuger and Speer bent over an architectural blueprint for the installation while Kreuger pointed out the finer points of the project.

Clustering around Hitler's emissary from Berlin and their commander, Kreuger's military engineers described the latest developments, filling in the gaps of Kreuger's narration.

The order to commence building the line of fortifications had come from none other than Adolf Hitler himself. The Führer had been so taken with the concept of breaking the Allied spearhead with a strategy of fortified gun emplacements and massive trenchworks that he had called in his chief architect immediately.

Previously Albert Speer had designed the classically inspired architecture of the Reich Chancellery and the grandiose sports and Reich Party rally complex at Nuremberg. Only recently he had completed plans for his greatest project yet, the Adolf

Hitler Museum of Aryan Art, to be constructed in Hitler's home town of Linz, Austria.

Speer well knew the Führer's obsession with underground fortifications. Beneath the magnificent burnished marble floor of the Reich Chancellery, where the Nazi Führer planned his military strikes and conducted affairs of state, lay a hidden network of fortified bunkers. Built to the most exacting standards possible, the bunkers were to be used in the event that the Führer and his mistress, Eva Braun, had to take cover from Allied attacks on Berlin.

To Speer, the indisputable fact was incidental to the fact that Hitler's plans seemed to work more often than they did not. A pragmatic man to the end, Speer held Hitler in awe as a miracle worker while personally deriding his madness.

Speer had launched into the task of designing the fortified defensive complex with his usual eagerness to solve a new technical challenge. The plans for the defensive network had been ready within days, and construction had commenced immediately under Speer's personal supervision.

In the company of Colonel Kreuger, Speer now took a walking tour of the installation. Most of the work was being performed by slave labor, recruited by corvée from the townspeople of nearby regions.

At this stage of the war, Wehrmacht troops were far too precious a resource to spare for projects such as this. There was an infinitely greater need for their fighting skills at the front.

Still, his hand-picked team of army engineers was supervising the work, and Speer saw that—as well as could be expected under the difficult circumstances—the work was proceeding quite rapidly.

The gigantic bunkers fashioned from poured concrete had been almost completely installed. Each afforded sufficient room to house a company of soldiers. The pillboxes jutting out above the surface of the ground could support machine-gun emplacements, giant mortars and even big howitzers.

The greatest problem for Speer and Kreuger was how quickly the job could be completed. Model's troops were valiantly staving off the massive Allied advances in the north of France as were Blaskowitz's in the south, and the badly stretched German lines were growing even thinner day by day. But it might yet work. Speer was satisfied at least that the job was proceeding well.

*"Heil Hitler!"* Speer barked as he saluted Colonel Kreuger and climbed into the Focke-Wulf Condor transport aircraft that was to fly him directly back to Berlin. He would deliver his personal report to the Führer, a report of yet another miracle of modern warfare made possible by the unparalleled genius of Nazi Germany.

**21**

*Sainte-Maxime, France*

Sergeant Joe Minnevitch sat in Colonel Hackett's office telling his story to the old man. Minnevitch had gone directly to the colonel when he'd returned to their own lines through the assistance of Marcel Dupré and his partisan band.

Hackett would want to brief General Patch personally on the new development that threatened the situation near Falaise. It was his ass, after all, that was now squarely behind the eight ball. The infantry spearhead into German territory had been Hackett's baby, so all the heat came down directly on his head.

Minnevitch knew as much and reasoned that as the debacle caused by the ambush of the special tactical force was a Thunderbird affair, Hackett might want to "keep it in the family," so to speak, and not let the Intelligence boys get their pound of flesh until later on.

"Here's where the Germans are building their emplacement network," Minnevitch told Hackett. "It's roughly a mile wide, big enough to stop any advance cold because of its strategic placement."

"And you mean to say you've actually gotten inside for a look?" Hackett asked again.

"Yes, sir, I did," Minnevitch replied. "The commandant even said I'd make a good Aryan."

"Is that right?" Hackett asked.

"That's right, sir. The Germans have recruited slave labor by the hundreds. They're building at a feverish pace, and from the appearances of things, the base is almost ready to go operational."

Hackett contemplatively rubbed his chin as he regarded the map of France, then clasped his hands behind his back.

"I've checked with G-2," Hackett said finally after a couple of silent minutes ticked by. "The Intelligence boys don't know jack shit about this Nazi installation. Sure, they've heard reports about it, but they haven't been able to get a single good recon photo. The word is that so far they're not completely certain it's not a Nazi deception strategy."

"It's real, all right, and the reason nobody can get aerial recon of the place is because the kraut's aren't dumb, sir. They've got the area well camouflaged during the day and blacked out as soon as they hear one of our night spotter planes coming," Minnevitch put in. "The Maquis partisan unit we ran into told us that the Germans make good and sure that nobody talks. The punishment for breathing a word about what's going on is summary execution."

"Okay," Colonel Hackett said with a nod. "The question now is what in Sam Hill do we do about it? I suppose calling in a squadron of Flying Fortresses and carpet bombing the entire area is not feasible."

"That's right sir," Minnevitch responded. "The way the krauts have it designed, no matter how many bombs are dropped, it wouldn't put a real dent in the installation. But my men and I have cooked up a plan that might work—with a hell of a lot of luck, that is."

"I'm open to any suggestion you might have, Sergeant," the colonel finally said, "as long as it's reasonably workable. The problem is that I might not have the final say in what ultimately happens. I'll have to run the plan past General Patch to get his approval, and he might shoot me down or turn it over to Intelligence completely."

"I understand that, sir." Then Minnevitch began outlining the plan as he got up and grabbed a pointer off the ledge of a nearby blackboard to show the colonel the basics of the operation. "We figure the only reasonable chance of neutralizing the base is with a ground-force assault before the big guns are installed."

"I understand the principle, Sergeant, but what I don't see is how we can accomplish this feat. The Nazis still control the area, and by all estimates our own forces won't break through for a while yet, easily enough time for the Germans to get their guns fully deployed."

"That's the whole point, sir," Minnevitch put in. "You see, our side already *does* have a force of trained men not far from the sea." He stepped up to the tactical map and jabbed his forefinger at a spot to the south of the installation.

"Stalag 20, sir," Minnevitch continued, tapping the map with his fingers. "There are something like two thousand battle-trained troops there, and many of them are Thunderbirds captured during the ambush at the farmstead."

Colonel Hackett's eyes widened as he suddenly comprehended what the NCO was telling him. What Minnevitch had in mind was nothing short of crazy, but Hackett had seen more craziness in this war than in the rest of his life combined. Right about now, crazy was actually beginning to sound good to him.

"You don't seriously intend to say you're suggesting using those men to stage a rear-guard attack on the Nazi installation, do you, Sergeant?" Hackett asked.

"First they would have to be liberated from the POW camp," he went on, thinking aloud as he paced the office. "And even if this bid were successful, they would somehow have to be armed and the attack would have to coincide precisely with a breakthrough from our spearhead forces."

"That's exactly right, Colonel," Minnevitch told the commanding officer. "What we're suggesting is that we use the ready-made force of POWs to sweep in and bust up that kraut installation. Our timing would have to be like clockwork, of course.

"But consider this, Colonel," Minnevitch continued. "With the Nazis losing the war in France, those POWs won't be long for the camp, anyway. They'll be brought to Berlin before too long, and once they're inside Germany, their lives won't be worth a plugged nickel. If they buy it on the battlefield, I for one would consider it to be an improvement."

"I see the whys and wherefores, but I still don't quite grasp the nuts and bolts of the operation," the colonel said as he paced about. "By what method would the men be liberated from Stalag 20 and in what manner would they be armed?"

"Just before, I mentioned the group of French Maquis we connected with, Colonel," Minnevitch replied. "The Frenchmen are ready to support the mission without reservation. They know every inch of the countryside and are willing to do whatever it takes to stop the Nazis.

"What we would need to do would be to paradrop a small unit near the stalag, make contact with the commanding officers of the camp and inform them of our plan. Then a second paradrop just before the breakout would place caches of weapons in the hands of the Maquis. The Frenchmen would distribute the arms and act as guides toward the installation."

"Sergeant, what you're proposing is going to bring down the wrath of God once I run it by Patch," Colonel Hackett informed Minnevitch. "But I do like the sound of your plan. However, I'll need some time before I can get a definite answer. I'll send for you when I know. By the way, Sergeant, just who would make up this behind-the-lines unit your plan calls for?"

"Yours truly, sir," Minnevitch answered right away, "and a few of my men."

"Somehow I had a feeling you'd say that. One more thing before you go, Sergeant," Hackett went on. "In my book your courage and resourcefulness puts you in line for a promotion. How would you feel about wearing a lieutenant's bars on your shoulders?"

It didn't take longer than three seconds for Minnevitch to decide he didn't want any part of being an officer. In his book any soldier above the rank of sergeant was already half a civilian.

"Give the bars to some other dogface, sir," Minnevitch told the colonel. "I already like the stripes I got on my sleeve just fine."

Grinning broadly, Colonel Hackett watched the NCO exit his office as he lit up his briar pipe and puffed contemplatively. He thought for a moment and then picked up the telephone on his desk. "Give me General Patch," he said, a few moments later in a voice now full of resolution.

WITHIN HOURS Minnevitch and his men had received their orders. The operation was a go. The colonel had explained that at first Patch had no intention of letting noncommando troops handle the mission, but Hackett had insisted on his own men doing the job.

The fact that Minnevitch and his troops had already worked with a partisan group familiar with the area was the deciding factor for Patch, who in the end did not hesitate to give Hackett the okay.

"You men requisition yourselves all the gear you'll need both for your penetration and for the paradrop," Hackett had told them. "We've already contacted the French Maquis. They are expecting the plane at 0300 hours. You are to report to the airfield by 0100 hours to board the plane. That's all, except good luck."

There was one sticking point that Hackett had to agree on before he got permission, though. Army G-2 had gotten wind of the plan, and pretty soon the OSS was itching to cut itself a slice of the pie. The final result was that an OSS man was assigned to tag along on the mission. The spy boy was to meet the dogfaces at the airfield just before takeoff.

Hackett now shook the hands of each of the Thunderbirds. He knew he was sending this volunteer force on a mission from which they might never return. Yet he also understood that these fine soldiers were determined to give their all for their country.

With time a precious commodity, Minnevitch and his crew headed for the company armorer's office bearing a signed requisition from Colonel Hackett. It gave them carte blanche to draw any weaponry they needed no matter how exotic.

In short order the Thunderbirds armed themselves with tommy guns and hundreds of spare clips filled with rounds of .45-caliber ammo. They also selected the gear that was to go on board the planes for the second drop, war matériel to arm the hastily recruited force of POWs from Stalag 20.

In addition to their weapons and ammo, they drew plenty of hand grenades and blocks of new demolition ordnance called plastic explosive, a blasting gelatin consisting of a latex base.

Suited up and ready, the squad arrived at the airfield at precisely 0100 hours. The plane was already revving up prior to takeoff, running through its final flight checks. The aircraft was a four-engine C-54 transport plane, a kind that had seen plenty of heavy use over the skies of France.

Minnevitch and his troops noticed that the plane sported the painting of a big three-leaf clover on either side of its nose assembly. The inscription beneath it read The Shamrock Express. Then the pilot came up and introduced himself.

"Hannigan's the name," he said, "But just call me Doc." Doc Hannigan was redheaded, with a boyish face and twinkling blue eyes that had a touch of the leprechaun in them. At first glance he was a dead ringer for Jimmy Cagney.

Like virtually every infantryman, Minnevitch didn't have too much of a liking for flyboys. In his opinion they were a bunch of pampered glamour boys who got less than their fair share of the grit but a whole lot more of the glory of war than they had coming to them.

No infantry soldier could expect to head back Stateside after flying a certain number of missions the way the flyboys did, nor did they have the good chow and the other perks the Air Force pilots got. The only thing a dogface had to look forward to was a thousand miles of mud, German bullets and probably dying young.

Nevertheless, Minnevitch took a shine to Hannigan right off. For some reason he seemed like a regular Joe—at least for a flyboy.

Hannigan had been fully briefed on the mission and was itching to play a hand in it. "Don't worry me, buckos," he said in a voice lilted with an Irish brogue, "old Doc's the best damned pilot in all of France, and The Shamrock Express is the best aircraft in the skies. I'll get you there in one piece."

After they climbed aboard the aircraft, Minnevitch took his seat on one of the benches set flush against the cabin bulkheads and looked around him. He didn't see hide nor hair of the OSS guy and hoped that he'd be a no-show. Minutes later, to the droning accompaniment of its four engines, the plane was airborne. Well, so much for the spy boy, Minnevitch thought to himself.

Just then, a stranger in khaki fatigues who Minnevitch had assumed was a crew member came out of the dimly lit cockpit. Sitting down beside Minnevitch, he extended his hand.

"Sergeant, my name's Dan Letchworth," he said. "I'm the guy from the OSS."

Seeing the blue-steel glint in the sergeant's eyes, Letchworth quickly added, "Sergeant, I'm the best man with explosives in this theater of operations, even if I do say so myself. Like it or not, you're gonna need my help to pull this mission off. As far as anything else goes, you're in complete command. Now, how about we shake on it?"

Minnevitch smiled. "Put 'er there, pal," he said. Grabbing Letchworth's hand, he shook it with a firm, vigorous grip, pleased to note that the lieutenant shook hands almost as well as a regular GI Joe.

## 22

Doc Hannigan pulled back the throttle and gained altitude as quickly as possible. On the lighted instrument panel in front of him, the altimeter needle moved steadily as the plane climbed to an altitude of twenty thousand feet.

The flyboy had no illusions about the danger the mission presented to himself and even more so to the soldiers going in behind enemy lines. The Germans continually kept watch on the skies, and a lone transport plane, lightly armed and armored and without fighter escort, would be a sitting duck for Messerschmitts or ground-based flak batteries.

Hannigan had a couple of things going for him, though. The first thing was the likelihood the enemy would be on the lookout for a bombing sortie instead of a lone plane. Only bad luck, such as running smack into a Luftwaffe air patrol or being spotted from the ground, would lead to detection by accidental means. But Hannigan was counting on the luck of the Irish.

Cruising at high altitude ceiling so the steady thrumming of the transport plane's engines would be practically inaudible to ground-based spotters was one way of getting around that contingency.

German Messerschmitts didn't routinely fly at this precise ceiling, either, so the risk of detection by a Luftwaffe patrol was also minimized.

The weather was another factor weighing in Hannigan's favor. Just before takeoff a storm front had begun to move in from the southeast. Great big fluffy cumulus clouds, stacked halfway to the moon by a low-pressure front blowing in from the Mediterranean, meant there would be plenty of opportunities to fly the plane through the cover of cloud banks.

The final thing Hannigan had going in his favor was the almost moonless night. The sky was overcast and dark, and a sliver of a moon floated in the gaps between the cloud cover like a pale twist of lemon in a pony of gin. As Hannigan reached his ceiling of twenty-five thousand feet, he began to think that maybe, just maybe, there was a slim chance of pulling this screwball mission off.

JUST AFT of the pilot's cockpit, the Thunderbirds sat out the monotony of the flight in the personnel compartment. Arrayed on benches along port and starboard bulkheads, Minnevitch, Letchworth, Mutt, Amboy, Haystacks, Kelso and the rest of the Thunderbirds who had originally escaped the Nazi ambush prepared themselves for the coming landing in occupied France.

There was no time to train this bunch of dogfaces in parajump techniques. But then again, there wasn't any pressing need to parachute into the landing zone. The Maquis had reported they were capable of marking off a large field near the operations area to use as a landing field by the transport plane.

Marcel Dupré and his French Maquis fighters would be waiting for them at the perimeter of the landing zone at 0300 hours.

When the plane was in sight, they would signal the all clear with three blinks of a flashlight. Two blinks meant that the mission had to be aborted. A single blink indicated that the plane was to circle in a holding pattern and await further instructions.

As the troops sat on their butts listening to the steady drone of the transport's four powerful engines, the men applied burnt cork to their faces to dull the shine of their skin.

Helmets were stowed away in field packs with the rest of the gear. For the clandestine landing, they would wear black watch caps to further reduce the chance of being observed. Instead of general-issue khakis, they were outfitted with special black battle garb for this phase of the mission. It would help them blend into the nocturnal forest environment.

A couple of minutes after takeoff, the copilot came around back bearing a thermos of hot coffee and poured for those who wanted some a waxed paper cupful of the fresh java.

"Ah, goes down as easy as a Pittsburgh whore on a Friday night," Minnevitch said as he laced his with brandy from Sainte-Maxime and passed the bottle around. The men drank their spiked coffee to the accompaniment of the drone of the plane's engines.

For the time being, there was nothing left to do but sit it out. To help break the monotony, Haystacks began passing around some French postcards. He said he'd taken them off a dead German.

They looked like the real McCoy, all right, what with bloodstains around the edges and all. The cards depicted a well-endowed peroxide blonde having what the Brits might call "naughty" fun with a big white stallion.

Looking at the blue postcard started Fontana thinking about his girlfriend, Earline. Her last letter to him promised that she was being faithful, but Fontana couldn't help but wonder if it was true. Earline had enclosed a snapshot taken by a Polaroid Land camera. There was an arm just visible at the edge of the frame. Whose fucking arm was that? Fontana had been wondering.

Maybe the guy she was making it with behind his back, he figured. That line of thought started Fontana thinking about guys doing every which thing with Earline. Fontana knew he had to put the kibosh on that kind of thinking pronto. It could screw up his mind and make him zig instead of zag at the wrong moment, which could easily get his ass splattered all over France. After almost cracking up before, he'd had to practically beg to convince the sarge to let him in on the action. No way was he going to screw up this time. No way.

Mutt had some other worries. His barber-pole-patterned appendage had been killing him for weeks, ever since his drunken thirty-six-hour leave in Naples. Mutt figured he had the clap, but he was too embarrassed to go see a doctor. The best he could hope for at this point was that it didn't fall off or get shot off.

Buddy Kelso couldn't get the words to a song he'd heard on U.S.O. radio before takeoff out of his head. They whirled around and around inside his brain to the beat of the steady drumming of the transport plane's engines. Sometimes that happened to him, though he could never figure out why. Kelso leaned back and allowed the tune and its lyrics to dominate his mind.

Before too long the pilot's voice crackled from speakers in the plane's public-address system.

"Thought you brave boyos of the Oklahoma National Guard would like to know that we're approaching the landing zone," Hannigan said into his mike.

Through the peasoup-thick vapor of the cloud bank, Hannigan could make out the mountains of France many hundreds of feet below, as well as the fields of farmsteads stretched out in a crazy-quilt patchwork of light and dark areas faintly lit by the moon and stars.

Navigating without benefit of lights meant there was always the possibility of collision, but the altitude at which Hannigan flew made it an unlikely occurrence. "Estimated time of landing is fifteen minutes," he said over the cockpit-to-cabin hookup.

Ten minutes after Hannigan's last announcement, on the soil of France below, Philippe heard the faint rumble of a plane approaching from the northwest. He nudged the sleeping form of Marcel Dupré on the ground beside him.

"Plane," he whispered. "Listen. She is coming in."

At once fully awake and alert, Marcel readied the flashlight he had brought with him in order to signal to the American plane.

As he hunkered in the forest underbrush at the perimeter of the large clearing in the woods, the partisan leader now distinctly heard the throbbing of the plane's powerful engines intensify with each passing second as his sharp eyes scanned the almost moonless night sky for a visual confirmation.

Then, when the pulsing of the engines seemed as though it was almost on top of him, Marcel could make out the outline of the aircraft eclipsing the faint stars.

Getting out his flashlight, Marcel pointed it toward the belly of the aircraft and pressed the switch three times, signaling an all clear.

From the cockpit of the C-54 transport, Hannigan spotted the three flashes originating from the darkened woods below and breathed a silent sigh of relief. Smiling as his copilot flashed him the thumbs-up, Hannigan pushed the stick forward to nose the plane down as he began to circle the clearing in a series of low, downward-spiraling sweeps.

When the transport aircraft was just skimming the treetops, Hannigan began to make his final descent. In the passenger cabin the Thunderbirds strapped themselves down against the bulkheads and watched the treetops speed by as the aircraft juddered in the turbulence of the black night air.

Minutes later they felt the first lurch of the landing gear touching terra firma as the plane began rolling forward. Hannigan applied reverse thrust on the propellers, and the four magneto engines took care of the rest, slowing the aircraft to a perfect, controlled stop.

Minnevitch was at the front of the line of Thunderbirds. Throwing open the cabin hatch, he saw the shadowed shapes of the Maquis members racing toward them across the open field. At the head of the welcoming committee was Marcel. He threw out his arms and embraced his American comrade with typical French gusto.

"It is good to see you, my friend," he said in his gruff voice. "I hope you have brought the stinking Bosch the presents we spoke of."

"Don't worry," Minnevitch answered. "Santa's got a special surprise package wrapped up nice and pretty for all his bad little goose-steppers."

"So long, me buckos, and may the luck o' the Irish be upon you," Hannigan shouted as he waved from the cockpit and turned the transport around to make the takeoff. "Don't forget to give Hitler a kick in the Axis for me."

Hannigan knew that the takeoff would be far riskier than the landing had been. The field was much shorter than he was at first led to believe. Squeezing what power he could out of the four overworked engines, Hannigan taxied his Shamrock Express toward the treeline.

At first it didn't look like the plane would gain enough lift to enable it to get airborne, but then at the last possible instant the aircraft gained altitude and rose over the treetops.

Wiggling its wings, the C-54 transport plane soared overhead, banked to the southwest and disappeared into the blackness of the night sky. The Thunderbirds and their Maquis liaisons wasted no time in disappearing into the protection of the dense woods.

Mission time was 0256 hours and counting.

**23**

*Sector Charlie-Easy*

The dogfaces gathered around Joe Minnevitch for a last-minute briefing in the woods where they had been joined by the band of French partisan fighters.

"We've already been briefed on the game plan, but I'll run it past you mothers one more time just for good measure," Minnevitch said to the circle of men around him.

"The plane's scheduled to make its paradrop at exactly 0120 hours tomorrow," he continued. "That gives us just under twenty-four hours to slip into the POW camp, liaise with the prisoners' senior officers, plant the demolition charges we brought along and get ready to stage the jailbreak of the century."

As full of risks as the mission was, new information Marcel had just received made it more vital than ever. Through his network of informants, Marcel had learned that the Nazis had stepped up their plans to march the Allied prisoners of war to Berlin.

According to the French resistance chief's information, the POWs could be moved out as early as the following day. The Nazis planned to muster the men out into the exercise yard in the forecourt of Stalag 20 and make a surprise announcement.

There would be no time for the prisoners to organize a credible resistance effort. They would be immediately moved out at gunpoint and marched until they reached their destination or dropped dead on the way.

If the Franco-American move to free the captured troops and turn them into a rear-guard fighting force was to be successful, then there was barely enough lead time before the Nazis began to march the POWs in the direction of Berlin and, inevitably, to their deaths at the hands of the Gestapo and the SS.

THE HILLS of the region were honeycombed with ancient caverns. Marcel and his men had scouted out one of them to use as a hiding place during the opening phase of the mission. The cavern was much like the one the Thunderbirds had occupied during their previous encounter with the Frenchmen, except for the absence of rock paintings on the walls.

The approaches to the cavern were guarded by sentry patrols made up of partisan fighters who were natives of the area. Having played in these woods since childhood, they had the ability to blend into the forest underbrush and become virtually invisible. No German patrol would ever be able to catch Marcel's band unawares, although they had tried often enough.

After the Americans had stowed their gear, chowed down on K-rations and shared some good local wine with the Maquis band, Marcel and Philippe took Minnevitch and Lieutenant Letchworth on a night patrol in the direction of the prisoner-of-war camp.

The four of them were to proceed toward Stalag 20 and enter by a secret underground tunnel that the POW escape committee had completed only days before. The prisoners had been hatching their own escape plans, and the tunnel stretched directly underneath the exercise forecourt of the camp, emerging a good thirty feet beyond the prison's perimeter fence.

Already informed via secret courier of the visitors they were to expect, Colonel Haversham and the other ranking Allied officers of Stalag 20 were awaiting the appearance of the emissaries dispatched from divisional headquarters at Sainte-Maxime.

As Marcel told it, though, there was some dissension in the ranks regarding the mission's viability. The officers of the stalag were split down the middle regarding the feasibility of the task at hand.

Roughly half of the POW officers were in favor of risking everything in a desperate scheme to escape from the camp, while the other half wanted to take their chances with the Germans, figuring that the war would be over soon anyhow and the enemy wasn't likely to ill-treat their prisoners for fear of war-crimes charges later.

Unquestionably they themselves would be Allied prisoners all too soon enough.

"FROM HERE WE MUST BE especially careful," Marcel whispered to Minnevitch when he had brought the band within sight of the camp. The unit was now perched on the edge of a wooded rise overlooking the camp perimeter. "We are close enough for the guard dogs to pick up our scent if we are not careful, and the sound of a man's voice carries surprisingly far."

From their vantage point in the woods just beyond the perimeter fence of Stalag 20, they could see that the Nazi POW camp was encompassed on all sides by a double border partition twenty feet high.

Four guard towers were spaced at compass points along its perimeter. The crow's nests were each manned by two guards. One German kept lookout while the other crouched behind a .50-caliber Browning machine gun mounted on a swivel stand to afford the blowback-driven weapon a wide arc of fire.

The main entrance to the stalag was manned by a guard post spacious enough for a detail of three storm troopers. In front of the guard post was a moveable barricade with yellow and black stripes. A Wehrmacht soldier with a Schmeisser MP-40 submachine gun slung over his shoulder stood in front of it, blowing on his hands and holding them above the fire in a discarded fuel drum to warm them against the night chill.

As the black-garbed men in the woods silently watched, they saw a soldier exit the guardhouse and exchange words with the man who was warming his hands near the flames.

Both of the Germans laughed, and then the one with the cold hands went inside the guardhouse. The replacement took up his position, and he, too, took advantage of the heat of the fire.

Located beyond the stalag's main gate was a forecourt approximately thirty yards wide and sixty yards deep. It was the spot where the troops fell in for the daily morning and evening head counts, took exercise, tended gardens and received orders from their Nazi keepers.

To the left of the forecourt was the section of the camp occupied by the German staff. The camp commandant's office was housed in an olive drab single-story building flying the swastika flag, as was the base motor pool, radio shack, mess hall and the barracks buildings for officers and enlisted men.

· Minnevitch paid careful attention as Marcel pointed out various details and also explained how they would go about entering the camp unnoticed.

"Just beyond the clearing there lies the exit of the tunnel excavated by the stalag's escape committee," Marcel told Minnevitch and Letchworth. "See if you can tell me where it is located."

"I can't see a lovin' thing," Minnevitch said, trying to stare through the darkness.

Marcel laughed softly.

"The location of the tunnel entrance is marked by a large boulder—see the one over there." Right away they spotted the boulder, right beside the stump of a big tree, but it was hard to pick out from the forest landscape without knowing where to look. "By moving aside the stump of a tree that has been placed beside it—voilà!—the mouth of the tunnel is revealed."

However, the perimeter of the camp was probed continuously by million-candlepower searchlight beams pouring from an enormous beacon unit mounted on a truck just inside the forecourt. The searchlight was extremely powerful, and its blinding beam swept unceasingly across the clearing, lighting the area as brightly as day.

From the guardhouse near the stalag's main gate or from the guard towers above the perimeter fence, the Germans would have little trouble in picking off any unauthorized personnel pinned down by the searchlight beams.

"For this reason we must move hastily," Marcel explained to the two Americans, removing a stopwatch from his pocket and setting it. "I have timed these beams. They sweep across the field every three minutes.

"I have estimated we are allowed two minutes to cross from our position to the tunnel entrance, and one minute to enter the tunnel and replace the tree stump in time for the next man. A single slipup, and we have had it."

Minnevitch and the OSS lieutenant understood and mentally prepared themselves for the difficult run. Philippe would be the first man to go.

As Marcel depressed the stud on the side of his stopwatch, the small, spry Frenchman sprinted across the field just as the searchlight beam swept to the edge of the forest, his lithe form moving with the ease and speed of a fox.

The wiry Philippe managed to push aside the stump and disappear into the black hole exposed beneath it, then replaced the stump at almost the exact instant the powerful searchlight beam crossed it again on its return circuit of the stalag's perimeter.

Minnevitch looked at Letchworth. The task was a lot harder than it appeared, he could tell at a glance.

"Damn," said the OSS man.

"You're next," Marcel said, nudging Minnevitch. "Get ready."

Minnevitch steeled himself and sprang from cover immediately after the searchlight beam swept past his position. As he ran all out across the open space, he kept his eyes on the beam that was sweeping around the perimeter of Stalag 20.

The beam had already completed a half circuit by the time Minnevitch was close to the tree stump. Sweating from exertion, heart jackhammering in his chest, he pushed aside the stump and dived into the hole feetfirst.

It was a hell of a tight squeeze.

Suddenly he could see the edge of the forest begin to light up. There was a metal handgrip on the bottom of the stump, but something was preventing him from moving it over the mouth of the tunnel. With a start, Minnevitch realized that he wouldn't have enough time to slide the stump across the hole.

"Pull, pull!" said a frantic voice behind him. Philippe had appeared from the shadows of the tunnel and was reaching up to assist the GI. His strength, added to the sergeant's, succeeded in closing the hole just as the searchlight beacon played across it.

The blood thundering in his ears, Minnevitch listened for any sounds in the darkness indicating that the Nazis had been alerted to the presence of spies in their midst. Long seconds crept past, and still the quiet of the night was not pierced by the barking of watchdogs or the voices of sentries shouting at intruders.

"That was a close shave," Minnevitch said.

"Start counting," Philippe instructed.

"When you have counted twice sixty, get ready to pull the lieutenant down. He comes next."

Minnevitch began counting. The seconds passed slowly, each clock beat ticking away with agonizing slowness. Then he finally heard the sound of footfalls overhead and braced himself.

Moments later the stump moved. Reaching up, he pulled Lieutenant Letchworth down the hole.

Marcel was the last man in. The Frenchman entered the tunnel as smoothly and effortlessly as Philippe had done on the first trip out. *"Allez!"* Marcel told them, producing a small pocket flashlight. "I believe we are expected."

**24**

Walking doubled over through the inky darkness, the four-man probe team proceeded along the tunnel. Their eyes quickly adjusted to the light conditions, and Minnevitch saw that the tunnel was shored up by wooden beams. Minnevitch had spent some time in coal mining country as a kid. He knew a little bit about mines and the way they were constructed.

Under the circumstances, he was sure the prisoners of Stalag 20 had done everything possible to make the tunnel work. Nevertheless, it looked to be as rickety as they came. The GI newcomers could hear the support beams creak as they went along and felt dirt sift down from the tunnel's roof.

Because the tunnel was so narrow and low, forcing the probe team to walk in single file, their progress was laborious and slow. To make matters worse, the dirt floor of the tunnel was filled with close to an inch of groundwater, which had leached in through the soil.

"Our position is now directly underneath the forecourt of the stalag," Marcel whispered, turning to those who walked behind him. "Please be most careful to make no sound, or there is a chance that the Bosch will hear us."

For the next fifteen minutes they moved with agonizing slowness to avoid making any noise. Finally, with aching muscles and after what seemed a much longer time, the probe team reached the point where the tunnel terminated.

By the light of Marcel's flashlight, they saw a cylindrical earthen-walled pit about ten feet wide and twenty feet high. A wooden ladder ran up one of the sides of the pit as far as the planking of what would be the floor of one of the barracks buildings.

"Stay here," Marcel told the group, and ascended the ladder. When he got to the top, he stretched out his hand and rapped out a recognition code on the floor planking overhead. Three long, three short, three long. Moments later the trapdoor above their heads creaked open in a spill of muted light like that made by flashlights.

"Come up," a British-accented voice whispered furtively from above.

One by one, with Marcel in the lead, the four-man probe team climbed the ladder and emerged in the middle of the officers' barracks of Stalag 20.

Although the barracks was dark, with only a dim distant glow provided by the rotating beams of the searchlight in the back of the beacon truck and lights strung across the grounds outside, the eyes of the four newcomers were already adjusted to the pitch-black darkness of the tunnel and they could see fairly well. Minnevitch had no trouble recognizing Smilin' Mike Calhoun and seeing the faces of several other unknown American and British officers.

These were the camp's two ranking officers, Colonel Colin Haversham and the American Major Wynn Robnett. Haversham had a long, thin English face but a nose like W. C. Fields.

The two Americans automatically saluted their ranking officers, who smartly responded with dour faces. Captain Calhoun dispensed with formality after he himself returned their salutes.

"At ease, gentlemen," Smilin' Mike said with a broad smile on his chiseled features as he clasped the hands of the Minnevitch and Letchworth, then he shook the hands of the two Frenchmen. "Glad to see you here."

Smilin' Mike felt a warm glow of pride fill him as he looked at his own men who had staked everything on a mad gamble to do the impossible. Come what may, Calhoun was prouder at that moment to be a member of the Oklahoma National Guard than he had ever been in his entire life as a military man.

"I say, chaps," Colonel Haversham put in, speaking in hushed whispers and brandishing his walking stick, "there's every possibility that bloody Jerry will have all our heads for cricket balls. What ruddy guarantee do I have that my chaps won't get their rear ends blown off for nothing more than a face-saving move by your Colonel Hackett?"

Although the officers' barracks observed the lights-out regulations imposed by the Germans and all the men appeared to be asleep, those men posted nearest the door and windows of the barracks were fully awake and alert. They would signal by coughs and sneezes at the approach of any trouble.

"I'm afraid we can't offer any guarantees, sir," the OSS lieutenant said matter-of-factly, his hard gray eyes locked with the colonel's in a measured stare. "That's why we've been sent here. General Patch is well aware of the risks he's asking you and your men to undertake in the name of victory. That's why he has informed us to make certain you're aware that compliance is strictly voluntary. Without your unanimous consent, we will abort the mission.''

"Well, rather, yes," Haversham answered, somewhat mollified. "But I'd bloody well like to know a bit more about the motive behind this sacrifice you're calling upon us to make. This secret Nazi installation I'm told exists—just how important is it to winning the show?"

"Knocking out the base and destroying its ability to hinder or stop our advance altogether is critical to the success of the drive to take France, Colonel," Minnevitch explained. "Colonel, I don't have to tell you how the Germans were able to go to ground in the Aurunci Mountains beyond the Salerno beachhead. What should have taken weeks took months. The same or worse could happen here if Hitler's plan works out. We can't afford to allow that."

"Quite right," said Haversham as he lit a cigarette and drew deeply. "Bloody foul German tobacco," he cursed, then said, "I see what you mean, Sergeant." Haversham looked questioningly at the American major, one eyebrow quizzically raised.

"What is your opinion?" he asked Major Robnett. "After all, it's your side that's dreamed up this bloody gamble."

"Colonel," Robnett began, "I don't see any other way than to give the operation our fullest possible support. I think I speak for my men when I say we will do what is expected of us, no matter what the cost."

Haversham shrugged like a man already resigned to a course of action.

"Then I suppose that says it all, gentlemen," he said dryly. "As commanding officer of the prisoners of Stalag 20, I think I can speak for every chap in this POW camp when I say that every man jack of us is with you in this bloody do. Now, how in heaven's name to you intend to break us out?"

MOVING STEALTHILY across the compound of Stalag 20, the four invaders planted blocks of plastic explosive at the points the sappers had briefed them to use. Here Minnevitch deferred to the OSS man's knowledge of demolitions and allowed Letchworth to call the shots.

It turned out that the Intelligence boy was as much of a wizard with the plastic stuff as he claimed, expertly slipping through the shadows between the perimeter patrols and slotting the charges at pressure points where they would do the most damage when the timing devices triggered the explosions.

Although the plastic charges would go up with a hell of a big bang, explosions were designed to be purely diversionary in nature, intended to get the Germans looking, running—and hopefully shooting—in the wrong direction.

The important damage would be done to the main gate of Stalag 20 by a few well-placed bazooka rounds.

The plan called for high-explosive 2.36-inch shells to blow the military prison camp's main gate. That action would commence as soon as Marcel's Maquis forces radioed the Americans that the paradrop had been completed and the weapons and ammo were ready to be distributed to the escaping prisoners along with fresh uniforms.

When Letchworth had slotted the demo charges, the four intruders shook hands with the commanders of the POWs and crawled through the escape tunnel. They succeeded in reaching the protection of the woods by the same difficult means they had used to reach the tunnel hours before.

It was just a little before dawn, and Hannigan's plane was not scheduled to return to the forest landing field until some time after midnight the following night.

This slack time would give the Americans and the Maquis the opportunity to catch a couple of hours' worth of much-needed shut-eye before they began final preparations for the mass POW escape. It was also a chance for each of them to make his peace with himself. Every man on the ground figured that before the run was over, his number might be up.

## 25

All was silent as Minnevitch, Marcel, Lieutenant Letchworth and the other members of the blacksuited probe team hunkered in the woods surrounding the site of their clandestine landing the previous night.

The time was now 0120 hours. Sergeant Joe Minnevitch sat with the flat of his back propped against the trunk of a tree and his butt ensconced between two big woody roots. He had the boxy transmitter of a special low-wattage radio unit sitting on the ground between his legs and he held on to the radio's handset while he twisted the dials with his other hand.

Transmitting its signal on a low-power waveband with a limited range of approximately six hundred yards, the radio beam was not likely to be detected by the mobile electronic listening posts that the Germans had deployed in the area.

The mobile listening posts were always probing the ether for signals Intelligence the Nazis could exploit to their advantage. Two units could quickly and efficiently triangulate a signal's source, in which case a patrol was sent out to apprehend those responsible. There was no way to be sure where the mobile listening posts were located, so sending even a brief radio message was highly risky.

When Hannigan flew the transport plane into receiving range, Minnevitch had to transmit the coded signal for the flight crew to go into action. Hannigan and his flyboys knew what they had to do once they received the ground crew's message.

If Minnevitch reported that the mission was a go, Hannigan was to drop the crates of ordnance and weaponry that were stacked up and ready to go against the bulkheads of the plane's cargo bay.

On the other hand, if the mission were aborted, the flyboy was to hightail it back to the divisional airfield at Sainte-Maxime. In that case the troops he had flown into the danger zone would be required to worry about getting their own asses back behind Allied lines under their own steam.

Laden down with rifles, ammo, grenades, bazookas and fresh uniforms for the escapees so heavily that takeoff had been difficult, the American C-54 transport plane was scheduled to pass overhead in just a few minutes.

Stroke by stroke, Minnevitch watched the luminous sweeping second hand of his wrist chronometer tick off the seconds, then the minutes, until finally he no longer needed the watch to inform him that zero hour had finally arrived.

Very clearly now, yet still just at the limits of human hearing range, the night fighters who were assembled at the edge of the woodland clearing could hear the steady drone of the four-engined transport aircraft's magneto-driven piston engines.

Hardly a moment later Minnevitch made visual contact with the aircraft. Pulling up the radio's long antenna, he flipped on the power switch, lifted the handset and began to transmit the prearranged coded message to the airborne support unit.

"Red Dog One to Red Dog Two," Minnevitch said softly and evenly, repeating the identification code once more, "Come in Red Dog Two."

"Red Dog Two, over." Hannigan's voice came over Minnevitch's headphones. "Good to hear your voice, me bucko. Awaiting message. Over."

"Little Boy Blue wants his Christmas shoes," Minnevitch growled into the mouthpiece. "Repeat, Little Boy Blue wants his Christmas shoes," Minnevitch said again slowly and distinctly. The message had been chosen because its consonants were clearly recognizable over the static-ridden airwaves.

"I copy that, Red Dog One." Hannigan's voice came back clearly over the transmitter's speaker. "Christmas shoes on the way. Good luck. Over and out."

The plane's engines took on a deeper pitch, roaring like some big jungle cat as the aircraft circled the clearing, ready to drop its cargo. Inside the cabin the cargo handler pushed the crates of war matériel out through the open hatchway just aft of the wings.

From the woods at the edge of the clearing, the hidden men who expectantly watched the night skies could see the black parachutes blossom against the star-spangled night sky.

Moments later the Maquis partisan fighters were running toward the crates with crowbars in their hands. Prying apart the crates, they filled their arms with as much of the lethal cargo dropped by the American plane as they were able to carry.

EVERYTHING WENT HAYWIRE all at once.

The German guards of Stalag 20 were rudely awakened from their sleep by the demolition thunder of plastic explosive charges going off.

Panic gripped the hearts and minds of the Germans while the Allied POWs greeted the harsh boom and roar of these diversionary explosions with the wild cheers of men exulting in the sound of their deliverance.

Fully briefed on the role they were to play in the mission to come, the POWs jumped the Wehrmacht guards stationed in each barracks building.

Arming themselves with captured guns and grenades and makeshift weapons that had been improvised for the bustout, the POWs surged from their barracks and stormed the prison compound, in the process commandeering more Schmeisser SMGs, Gewehr assault rifles and even an MG42 light machine-gun taken from a gun emplacement.

As the larger body of unarmed troops hurled themselves vengefully on the Germans, a smaller force of officers and some enlisted men awaited the second explosive report signaling that the camp's main gate was shattered to smithereens.

When this occurred they would spearhead the charge to freedom. Only minutes later they heard the roar and thunder of the exploding bazooka rocket rounds ripping the night asunder, and raced full tilt toward the front of the camp.

The Nazi guards were already pouring out of their barracks in droves, and the machine gunners in the crow's nests on the camp perimeter trained their heavy-caliber chatterguns on the prisoners who now totally overran the Nazi base.

White-hot dots and dashes stitched downward through the blackness of night as .50-caliber tracer bullets rotored from the machine guns in the crow's nests above the compound.

Scores of prisoners were immediately cut down in midstride by the swaths of automatic fire lancing down from above and by the small-arms fire sent blasting their way by storm troopers streaming from the barracks longhouses in a deadly torrent of Nazi gray.

But the prisoners were motivated by desperation, and therein lay their strength. For every man of them cut down by rotoring German lead, two more came on at a run, heedless of the fire directed toward them, living just long enough to rip the guns from the hands of the Germans and shoot them down with their own weapons.

In no time flat the human wave of men who once again had been given the chance to die on their feet like soldiers was surging in a bloodstained tide through the gaping rupture torn in Stalag 20's main gate by the roaring fire of the Yank bazooka.

Outside, beyond the flame-curtained perimeter of the POW installation, the Maquis forces were awaiting their arrival, ready to hand out weapons and ammunition to every man they could arm.

The Frenchmen had loaded as many of the rifles with full clips as possible and had dumped the stiff new uniforms on the ground in enormous heaps. Shouting instructions above the din of raging battle, they directed the soldiers to the war matériel flown in by Hannigan and his crew.

Overwhelmed by the sheer force of numbers, the Germans brought up two armored cars and a tank to take on the escapees. The tank was a Panzer Mark IV armed with a no-nonsense howitzer cannon.

With the savage tolling of man-made thunder, the Panzer hurled its deadly high-explosive shells into the camp. Fire and shrapnel ripped great gaps in the POW lines until a squad of prisoners armed with a bazooka succeeded in turning the tank into a blazing steel pyre, most of its Nazi crew torn apart and the rest taken prisoner.

Still the Spandau machine guns chattered from the tracked armored cars, and men with bodies ripped asunder fell to die in the dirt beneath the full-auto fury of steel-jacketed German vengeance.

Under the direction of Calhoun and other officers, the prisoners organized a grenade charge to deal with the mechanized German armor. Forming up into two offensive lines, one carrying hand grenades with their cotter pins already pulled while the other held Garand rifles at the ready, they got ready to give the enemy a dose of their own bitter medicine.

On Smilin' Mike's command, the rifle brigade commenced shooting at the armored cars, massing their fire and forcing the machine gunners to tuck their heads down. As soon as the firing ceased, the second line of troops, carrying the grenades, rushed forward and hurled their lethal pineapples at the war wagons to devastating effect.

*Boom! Boom! Kahhhh-Boooom!*

Rolling underneath, bouncing between their treads, thudding into the firing ports in their steel-plate hulls, the grenades ripped ragged gashes in the armored chassis of the German war wagons and blew their wheels right out from under them.

Through thick clouds of acrid battle smoke rising from the burning armor, badly wounded Germans crawled with their hands in the air and pleas for mercy on their lips, to be captured or killed outright by the victorious POWs.

Though it cost a stiff toll in lives, the tactic soon put every armored car out of commission just as quickly as the tanks. Soon, from out of the original chaos of the escape, the prisoners were the ones in control of Stalag 20.

## 26

Among the captured Germans from Stalag 20 was its commanding officer, Colonel von Schmundt. Although he was now a prisoner of war himself, von Schmundt still sneered down his long patrician nose at the Allied soldiers who had succeeded in turning the tables on their brutal Nazi masters.

It made no difference to von Schmundt which side had won the battle. A Nazi was always a Nazi, even in defeat. As an officer of the German Reich and an Aryan, as well, von Schmundt considered himself to be far superior to his captors.

The Maquis partisan forces marched von Schmundt away at the head of a column of disarmed troops. What the fate of the captured German soldiers would be at the hands of the Frenchmen whom they had persecuted for so long was not the affair of the Thunderbirds.

Their mission only involved securing the German base and holding their positions until relieved. As far as the dogfaces were concerned, the problem of what to do with the German prisoners had been solved for them. Whatever happened to the enemy, they probably deserved everything they got.

With the camp secured, the OSS man, Lieutenant Letchworth, set a couple more demolition charges, scattering them here and there across the camp perimeter. The ordnance detail he'd set up wired the charges together and strung the cables to a detonator box. Letchworth attached the leads to the box and screwed in the plunger. Then, with a final look at the stalag, he pushed down hard.

Explosions boomed and echoed as pillars of fire and columns of smoke shot upward from the demolition zone, throwing hot spinning embers everywhere like the spray from some hellish fountain.

As the blast's echoes died away, the prisoner-of-war camp became engulfed in a cauldron of scorching, licking flames. The crackling and howling of the blazing inferno that devoured the wooden barracks buildings was visible for miles around and would quickly bring a German relief column heading right for its position.

The likelihood of such a development was already factored into the assault force's battle plans, though. At any rate, soon the issue would be academic. The escaped prisoners of Stalag 20 would be on the march, long since gone from the area.

Wearing new uniforms, cleanly shaven and fed by the rations dropped by Hannigan and what they had been able to promote from German stores, the troops were refreshed and eager to move from a place that held nothing but bitter memories for them.

Formed up into platoons under the direction of the ranking POW officers, the troops formed infantry columns and commandeered Nazi staff cars, weapons and whatever mechanized armor could be salvaged and pressed quickly into service.

Hastily outfitted in this way, their morale high, the American and British POWs began their march to-

ward the Nazi installation that was to be the target of
their rear-action strike.

Each man among this ragged but determined force
knew about the tremendous sacrifices that were
expected of him in the coming battle. Yet every soldier was prepared to accept the ultimate penalty, give
the ultimate sacrifice and contribute to the ultimate
victory over the hated Germans.

At the head of the column marched the Oklahoma
Guardsmen. The Thunderbirds were out to avenge the
Germans who had ambushed them and slaughtered
their brothers in arms. They would be damned to hell
before taking second place in the coming assault to any
man, no matter what his nationality. The Oklahomans were ready to tangle with the Germans, ready to
pay them back a hundredfold for what had been done
to them.

Acting as the force's guides, the French partisan
fighters went on ahead of the infantry column, scout-
ing ahead for signs of trouble, making certain there
would be no deadly surprises in store for the men who
marched behind them.

Marcel Dupré and his brave Maquis fighters were
intimate with every square mile of the territory
through which the column moved. Bivouacking by day
and marching mostly by night to avoid detection by
enemy patrols on the ground and spotter planes in the
air, the French partisans managed to bring the raid-
ing force within striking distance of the installation
without being spotted by enemy patrols.

But the Germans were not standing by idly. They
were eager to find the escaped prisoners and doubled
their patrol strength in the forest. On the second night

of their march, Marcel and his band happened upon a patrol bivouacked in the woods.

The partisans noted that the patrol included an armored car and two motorcycles with attached sidecars. These vehicles would make excellent additions to the mechanized armor already taken from Stalag 20.

Intent on taking the valuable prizes undamaged and not wanting to fire on the Germans—a firefight was sure to draw more of them to the area—the Maquis scouts unsheathed the long bayonet knives that hung from their waists.

"Yves, Jacques, do it quietly," Marcel whispered to his comrades.

"As silent as death, my friend," Yves returned, and Jacques only smiled a killer's smile. Splitting up, the partisans melted into the shadows. Sneaking up on the sentries walking their perimeters on the edge of the encampment, the Frenchmen began to perform their bloody work.

Treading softly on the loamy ground without so much as the snapping of a twig to give him away, Marcel took out his German sentry. Springing from cover, he put his left hand over the Nazi's mouth to keep him from crying out and with the other hand plunged the point of the bayonet into his throat.

Yves and Jacques took out their sentries just as silently and expertly as their leader had done. But Jacques was more savage in the manner by which he dispatched his Nazi.

Getting behind the sentry, clasping his hand over his face, Jacques plunged the bayonet tip into his side again and again, thrusting in the dagger until he was covered with the blood of the hated enemy, then let the dead German slump lifelessly to the ground.

Moving like ghosts, the partisans slipped into the encampment, where two more soldiers slumbered soundly on Wehrmacht-issue bedrolls. Jacques's dark form loomed menacingly over the sleeping men.

He was ready to send them into sleep everlasting.

He slit the throat of one of the sleeping Germans, seeing the German's eyes bugging just before they glazed over and he went limp forever.

The second man was still sound asleep, and Jacques wiped the blade of his knife on the dead Nazi's greatcoat and silently slid a blackjack filled with lead buckshot out of his jacket pocket.

Bringing the blackjack savagely down on the sleeping man's skull, Jacques knocked him unconscious, then, working quickly, he placed the dead body on top of the senseless man and lashed them together with strong rope. When the German awakened, a nasty surprise would be waiting in store for him.

Marcel tapped Jacques on the shoulder. "Enough of this, let us go." He thought Jacques did these jobs with an excess of enthusiasm, but he knew the enemy had done far worse—and to innocent women and children. He understood well how the kind of hatred Jacques felt could twist a man inside, but encouraging such behavior would do Jacques no good.

Sending Jacques ahead to advise the Americans and British soldiers that they would be driving the captured German vehicles to the encampment, Marcel ordered his men to climb on board and start the engines.

*Sector Able-Bravo*

NOW THEY WAITED. In the night they had dug trenches in the forest floor and settled in for what was to come next.

Just as the sky lightened with the coming of day, the rumbling of the bomber squadron roaring up from bases in Northern France could be heard in the distance.

The big B-17 Flying Fortresses carried hundreds of pounds worth of blockbuster bombs. The bomb crews had already chalked and painted their favorite slogans on the bombs. Many of the bombs destined to smash the Nazi base carried pinups of Betty Grable taped to their casings. Others bore likenesses of Hitler, Mussolini and Göring.

Minutes later the entrenched force of ex-POWs saw the sky grow black with the bomber formation as they heard the Klaxons warn the Germans in the installation to take cover from the coming rain of bombs.

Soon, ack-ack guns set up a flak front, but still the big Flying Fortresses came on. They roared over the target until they were in bombing range, swarming overhead like gigantic bumblebees, their stingers dripping poison, ready to be thrust directly into the heart of the Nazi war machine.

Then, when they were finally over the target, the bombardiers let fly the high-explosive blockbuster bombs. Each plane was loaded to drop a stick of many bombs on the target.

Lighter when their bomb bays were empty, the aircraft would turn around and head back to their bases

up north, escorted by a wing of P-38 fighters to protect them against attacks by German Messerschmitts.

With the number of planes in the bomber squadron, several tons' worth of high-explosive bombs
would strike the target almost simultaneously. Enough
ordnance to blow the base to hell and back again.

*Wheeeerrrrrr-BLAMMMM!*

*Wheeeerrrrrr-BLAMMMM!*

Tumbling through space, the bombs sang out their
vengeful song of death before striking with a thunderous explosion that made the ground tremble and
shudder violently as they detonated on their target,
smashing it to pulverized, burning rubble.

The poured-concrete pillboxes erected by the German assault engineers and their slave laborers were
demolished instantly, and the base's ammo and fuel
dumps went up in roiling, churning, clouds of foul
black hellsmoke.

*Wheeeerrrrrr-BLAMMMM!*

*Wheeeerrrrrr-BLAMMMM!*

When the last bomb had screamed its way to earth
and left its fiery signature behind, the big Flying Fortresses banked and flew off, their crews knowing that
the heart of the installation was still intact despite the
savage pounding the Nazi base had been subjected to.

It was time for the ground forces dug in beyond the
zone of destruction to sweep into the rubble and deliver the final blow. At last the moment of reckoning
had arrived for the Germans.

As for the Thunderbirds, it was the moment of
long-awaited revenge.

## 27

"Onward, lads! For King and Country! For the red, white and blue!" Colonel Haversham shouted into the mike of the communications unit. "Give bloody Jerry a thrashing he'll long remember!"

Using the captured Panzer tank and armored carriers against their former owners, the newly freed POWs rushed forward in a two-pronged attack on the Nazi stronghold.

Within the installation, chaos reigned supreme. Just beginning to recover from the shock of the surprise bombing raid, the German forces were dazed and disoriented.

Colonel Kreuger was covered with plaster dust from head to foot, and his ears still rang from the terrifying din of the blockbuster bombs dropped by the roaring B-17 bombers.

An aide hurried to his side, bringing even worse news.

*"Herr Oberst,"* shouted the aide, terror making his eyes glow with an inner light. "There is a force of Americans and Englishmen closing fast on the installation."

"Where do they come from?" Kreuger demanded.

"I do not know," the aide answered. "Only that there has been an escape from Stalag 20, east of Le Mans. As yet there is no further information available on the nature of the escape."

"Did you get through to Châteaudun garrison before the set malfunctioned?" Kreuger asked, turning to his radioman, who sat twisting dials on the communications apparatus console.

"I believe so, *Herr Kommandant,*" the radioman responded with Prussian crispness, turning in his seat to face the colonel.

"Damn you, *schweinehund!*" Kreuger yelled with spit flying from his mouth, no longer able to contain his rage at the blow he had been dealt. "I don't want 'maybes'! Did you or did you not?"

The radioman swallowed hard, intimidated by his commanding officer's rage and mortally afraid that he would be shot on the spot. It had been known to happen when the colonel hadn't been answered correctly.

"I cannot say with complete certainty," he stammered. "Atmospheric conditions were not good. But I am ninety percent certain that the request for a relief column did get through."

Kreuger contemplated a bit, staring at the radioman with eyes that seemed to bore right through his skull. "All right, private," he finally said. "What about now? Have you repaired this *verflucht* contraption yet?"

"*Herr Kommandant,* I am trying. The transmission unit has suffered some severe damage due to the effects of the American bombing. However, I am close to getting it working again. This I can state with complete confidence."

"Very well, then," Kreuger replied, somewhat mollified. "As soon as the radio is operational, repeat your request for a relief column and get confirmation. Is that understood?"

*"Jawohl, Herr Oberst!"* the radioman barked in reply, greatly relieved that the colonel's homicidal wrath had not been vented on him. For the time being, at any rate.

Kreuger had a great deal to think about and very little time in which to do his thinking. The Allied prisoners were now engaging in a pincer movement with the intention of overrunning the installation.

As matters now stood, they had a fair chance of accomplishing their objective. The colonel's own forces were spread thinly. Reports from every corner of the base were coming in all the time. The Flying Fortresses and their American bombs had smashed the fortifications utterly, beyond hope of repair.

The German base's ammo supplies had gone up in flames, and their armored vehicles were out of commission, along with many of the big guns, which had been blown clean off their emplacements.

Due to the high-level damage inflicted by the lightning-swift bombing strike, the battle to take the installation would be one largely of infantrymen against infantrymen.

In this crucial respect, the escapees from Stalag 20 enjoyed the advantage of having absolutely nothing left to lose and absolutely everything to gain by victory, regardless of its cost in lives and matériel.

"Order the troops to engage the enemy," Kreuger shouted at his aide, drawing his Mauser pistol and checking its clip. "Tell them to hold their positions until they are relieved."

*"Jawohl, Herr Oberst!"*

"Any man who tries to surrender will be shot like a dog!" continued Kreuger. "Make certain all officers and enlisted men understand this order well. They are to hold until relieved. Under no condition is there to be any surrender!''

*"Jawohl, Herr Oberst!"* the red-faced aide yelled at the top of his lungs, and spun on his heels to leave the bunker.

Colonel Kreuger next turned toward the radioman. He cocked the pistol, chambering the first parabellum round, and pointed the Mauser at the radioman's head.

"You have five minutes to raise the garrison at Châteaudun and get a relief column on its way," he said evenly. "After that I will blow your brains out."

The Wehrmacht radioman quickly turned back toward his equipment, frantically working the dials even though he knew full well that he could sooner make contact with the angels in heaven than raise Châteaudun garrison on his malfunctioning rig.

**28**

Through the shattered concrete rubble, the acrid, billowing smoke and the stench and the blood and the deadly crackle of automatic fire, the Thunderbirds surged across the blasted ruins of the Nazi installation.

The Nazi forces, though knocked back on their heels by the one-two punch of the unexpected attack, had rallied quickly and had effectively reorganized their ranks to meet the assault.

Following standard Wehrmacht combat doctrine, they had turned the devastation of the rubble produced by the bombing raid into effective defensive positions.

Raw fear helped bring discipline to their ranks and accuracy to their fire. Men threatened with field executions were capable of working miracles, Colonel Kreuger had long ago discovered.

From out of the broken ruins the Allied air raid had made of the Nazi base, the German Wehrmacht had fashioned fortified positions that could be defended to the last man.

Colonel Kreuger had drilled his storm troopers well.

Though still dazed from the bombing, many of them severely injured in the attack, the German storm troopers had deployed machine guns, mortars and rifle crews to meet the coming onslaught.

Even as the Thunderbirds and the remainder of the American, British and Canadian forces stormed across the no-man's land at the perimeter of the base to wrest the soil of France from Hitler's grasp, the Nazi forces were counterattacking.

Minnevitch, Mutt, Haystacks and Amboy found themselves going up against a well-sited machine-gun nest. Minutes later they were joined by privates Conners, Wright and Dugan. The Nazis had expertly manned the fire emplacement. Using a large shell hole that was easily twenty feet in diameter, they had deployed a tripod-mounted 7.92 mm MG42 light machine gun.

Around the emplacement they had spread large chunks of shattered rubble to afford the position greater protection from the Allied assault. The German machine gunner crouched behind the tripod-mounted MG42, his hand clutching the pistol grip so hard his knuckles whitened. The first 7.92 mm round was already in the chamber, and the trooper by his side was ready to feed the belt of ammo into the gun's receiver.

Hunkered behind the MG42, his eyes hollow, his tensed jaw muscles twitching with spasms, the machine gunner continued to wait until the force of khaki-clad figures came within the lethal range of the air-cooled burp gun.

"Soon, soon, Hansel," he spoke to his weapon, caressing its perforated barrel and smelling the fresh coating of oil that he had carefully applied to each part of the broken-down gun during a recent cleaning. "Just a little more, Hansel, just a little..."

Suddenly, making a sound that was a combination of a madman's laugh and the snarl of a cornered animal, the German gunner triggered the first long burst of Krupp steel. His laugh became a shrill battle cry as he felt the MG42 buck in his hands and inhaled the stinging sharpness of the combined smells of overheated gunmetal and flash-igniting primer.

The air became alive with whirling, mangling steel and the banshee scream of the staccato death knell of automatic fire as yellow hell flames belched from the bell-shaped muzzle of the light machine gun.

Caught across the beltline by a brace of spinning rivets, Private Billy Wright spread out his arms as though he were ready to take off from the face of the earth like a bird in flight. But the only place his newly minted angel's wings took him was straight to the bottom of hell.

"Down!" Minnevitch shouted as Wright hit the dirt, skidding on his face in a tangled heap, dead before he hit the ground. Dugan took a hit in the leg from another automatic burst, and he crumpled to the shattered rubble of the ground, where he lay moaning.

Yelling for Mutt to cover him, Minnevitch dared the Reaper as he dodged German bullets and succeeded in dragging Dugan to the cover of a shell hole, barely able to outpace the flying line of slugs as the machine gunner tracked his weapon on them.

"Mary and Joseph, was that ever a close shave!" Mutt shouted. Still more 7.92 mm bullets raked the lip of the crater, screaming and whining as they ricocheted off rocks and rubble and forced the men inside to cower like rats. And then, suddenly and without warning, the shooting abruptly stopped.

"You want to take a look or should I?" asked Mutt.

"Uh-uh," Minnevitch returned.

Mutt shrugged. Then he took off his steel pot helmet and propped it on the end of his rifle butt. Holding the rifle by the end of its barrel, he lifted the helmet above the lip of the crater. It rang like a Chinese gong as the trigger-happy gunners opened up with a short burst of 7.92s.

"I've had a bellyful of this crap," Minnevitch cussed. Without further ado, he pulled the pin from a hand grenade and chucked it stiff-armed over the lip of the shell crater. Seconds later it detonated with a loud *crump!* Again the machine gun fell silent, and the Thunderbirds taking cover in the shell hole heard the Germans shouting at each other frantically.

Minnevitch didn't like the ominous silence holding sway after the shouted exchange. He knew something worse than the machine-gun fire that had killed Wright and wounded Dugan was waiting in the wings.

*WHUPPPP!*

Minutes later the earth trembled as if a giant had stomped it in anger, and Minnevitch realized that the Germans had either brought in a mortar detail to settle their hash or had radioed to a mortar pit nearby to commence dropping rounds on their position. More than ever they were like rats in a hole where they were taking cover.

Minnevitch got out his remaining grenades and lined them up on the floor of the crater until he had eight all in a row.

"Mutt, you and Amboy keep me covered."

"Check, Sarge."

Minnevitch next pulled the pins from each grenade, arming them all. The metal spoons that held the firing pins securely in place were still attached, but would come loose when the fragmentation bombs were thrown. Seconds later the grenades would detonate.

"Go!" Minnevitch shouted, and grabbed a grenade in each hand. Standing up and risking exposure to fire, he heaved with all his might and then quickly tucked back down in the cover of the shell hole. Before the twin explosions boomed and thundered across the battlefield, Minnevitch had already picked up two more grenades and threw them in quick succession, then repeated the action.

Carrying his final two pineapples, he jumped from the crater and ran hell-bent for leather toward the gun pit, daring the burning lances of German steel pounding his way from the machine gun's death-spitting barrel.

The Germans in the fire pit were stunned and reeling from the succession of grenade explosions and had trouble sighting their highly mobile target through the acrid clouds of battle smoke. In another second they would open up with the MG42, Minnevitch knew, and he'd be close enough so they couldn't possibly miss, but it was the only shot he had and he wouldn't get another.

Minnevitch kept on running toward the blazing muzzle of the MG42, wondering why he had not yet been hit by Nazi fire. Just before he was on top of the pit, he jumped up into the air and pitched the hand grenades into the gun emplacement.

Then he tucked to one side, rolling like a log to get as far away from the detonation zone as possible, and heard the twin convulsions of the grenades going off behind him.

Moments later the 7.92 mm ammo in the MG42's belt magazines cooked off, and there was a secondary explosion. A ball of incandescent gases rose into the air from the machine-gun emplacement, leaving nothing behind but charred body parts and flash-melted slag.

"Nice going, Sarge," Mutt applauded Minnevitch as he joined him moments later and handed over his tommy gun. Minnevitch was quickly on the run again, dodging renewed enemy fire.

He had just eyeballed a couple of Germans ducking into one of the shattered concrete blockhouses that had not been completely flattened in the bombing strike.

One was an officer, and if Minnevitch wasn't mistaken, it was the same colonel who had given him the Cook's tour of the installation. Not that there was any way that the colonel would ever recognize him in his GI issue and with his mug filthy with battle grime.

Guns readied, Minnevitch and his GI squad hustled after the fleeing enemy. But the officer had seen the doughfoots, too, and the second they were inside after him, the dogfaces ran right smack into the stream of chattering fire blazing from the German fisted gun.

During the second they caught sight of him up close, the squad saw for sure that he was the same Wehrmacht colonel and also noticed he packed a mean-looking Mauser machine pistol. The second soldier was somewhere up ahead.

The colonel wasted no time in snapping off a long burst of 7.63 mm lead. The burst forced the pursuing Americans to jump for the nearest cover as he hot-footed it into another doorway inside the bunker and down a flight of stairs beyond.

Minnevitch, Conners and Mutt flattened on either side of the entranceway and tossed grenades into the dark cavity yawning beyond it. The grenades went thunk-thunk-thunk down the stairs, and then there was a loud explosion as they detonated almost simultaneously.

Taking cover as the grenades went off with a deafening bang, the crew of Thunderbirds were mobile again in the moments following the reports of the exploding grenades. Each GI had the feeling that he had gotten lucky. This could be the installation's command center, and it was theirs for the taking.

Colonel Hasso Kreuger saw the Americans wielding their tommy guns and racing down the stairs hot on his tail. He grabbed the Nazi storm trooper whom he had just caught up to and used him as a human shield while the Mauser machine pistol in his hand belched fire and lead.

Mutt returned a stuttering burst of .45-caliber steel from his tommy, whipping the SMG's muzzle back and forth and feeling it buck in his fists. He caught the storm trooper full in the belly, chewing apart the man's stomach and opening up a dozen blood-spurting gashes.

Kreuger dropped the dead man and got off another burst of Mauser fire to force the Americans to take cover, then scurried farther into the vast bunker complex.

At the end of a corridor that stretched beneath the complex was located a fail-safe mechanism designed by Speer at Hitler's insistence. Deep within the base were charges made up of hundreds of pounds of TNT capable of blowing the entire complex sky-high.

On the Führer's direct instructions, not a trace of the installation was to be permitted to fall into the hands of the enemy. It would be blown to smithereens in the event that capture was imminent.

Since the unthinkable had come about and the base was about to be lost, Kreuger would blow it to hell and gone. As for his own fate, he had an escape exit that was for the personal use of Nazi officers.

The Nazi elite enjoyed better treatment than did the ordinary Wehrmacht troops, and Speer had been only too happy to carry on the tradition by designing the tunnel for the commandant's personal use.

The French slave laborers who had constructed this section of the base had been shot in the head as soon as it was completed in order to prevent any but loyal Nazis from learning of its existence.

All Kreuger needed to do now was to unlock the armored switch box and pull down the stirrup-shaped lever that armed the preset timing device. Then the demo charges would blow like hell, and nothing but burning ashes would remain behind for capture by the Allies.

He fished in his pocket for the keys that would unlock the box, painfully aware of the staccato clamor of automatic-weapons fire in the concrete corridor behind him, fire that grew closer and closer with every passing second. Sweat beaded his face, but Kreuger maintained the concentration of a true Nazi officer, his mind focused on nothing but the task he needed to perform.

Soon Kreuger had gotten out the key and was turning it in the lock. The latch flipped open, and his fingers gripped the fluted edges of the detonator timing dial. He armed the charges with two precise, savage twists of the dial, setting the mechanism for a detonation delay of five minutes. The only task left to be done was arming the bomb with a pull of the stirrup.

Suddenly the Thunderbirds appeared in the chamber's entranceway. It was fitting that there were witnesses to his final glorious act, thought Kreuger. Once the device was armed, they would not be able to stop the countdown to destruction anyway.

Kreuger understood he could not hope to escape the conflagration alive. But the Nazi felt he could meet death in peace knowing that the thousand-odd men who were fighting topside would also be killed in the apocalypse that would soon obliterate the entire zone. As for his own troops, they would die for the greater glory of the fatherland and the glorious German people as their Führer had every right to demand of them.

*Kreuger yanked the stirrup.*

## 29

"Hold it right there!"

In an instant Minnevitch had grasped what was about to happen. He figured that the Nazi was attempting to arm some kind of booby trap, and he also realized there might not be any way to stop the countdown sequence once the booby trap was armed.

There wasn't any question in his mind whatever. If the colonel was not stopped quickly, then the lives of every man in the area wouldn't be worth a plugged nickel.

Having already loaded a fresh clip into his special-issue Mauser machine pistol, though, Kreuger was snapping off 7.63 mm bursts as he clutched the handle of the lever with his left hand and prepared to pull it completely down, arming the detonation charge.

"Idiots! Fools!" Kreuger shouted maniacally as the Mauser barked and chattered in his fist. "You can never succeed! Even in death the pure-blooded German master race will annihilate you utterly!"

At that moment the Mauser's chamber port ejected its final shell casing. Its magazine was now empty, and the pistol would no longer fire.

The three GIs were prepared to jump the colonel, but Kreuger had a surprise waiting in store for them. With a demented shriek he produced a grenade and held it aloft.

The German antipersonnel munition was unlike the standard German potato-masher type or the American Mk2A1 type. The spoon-type detonator was similar to the Mk2A1, but the ordnance casing of the grenade was a large cylinder. The dogfaces could see that the grenade was missing the cotter pin that held the spoon in place.

"This is a phosphorus grenade," Kreuger cautioned them. "If I drop it, the room will be engulfed in flame. I do not think you will be able to reach me before I complete my mission, after all."

Momentarily stunned, the GIs backed off, except for Private Conners. He broke from the doorway and propelled himself into the room as though driven by the devil.

"Conners, stop!"

Minnevitch reached out for Conners, but it was already too late to stop him. Reacting instantly, the Nazi pitched the grenade. It bounced as it landed, then began rolling toward the dogfaces. As it wobbled across the floor, Conners flung his body directly over the incendiary bomb.

"Get the kraut—" he yelled.

Then, with a muffled boom and a brief, bright sudden flash, the grenade exploded.

A cocoon of blinding fire and acrid smoke enveloped Conners as the white phosphorus burst into flame. Conners screamed in agony and staggered to his feet, his body wreathed in scorching tongues of crackling fire.

Minnevitch had a split instant to chose between going to Conners's assistance or getting the German who had pitched the grenade. He knew what the decision had to be the instant the choice had presented itself.

"You dirty bastard," Minnevitch shouted, then sprang forward. From somewhere behind he heard Mutt holler a warning and saw the Nazi raise a small Walther pistol he'd pulled from a holster at his boot and fire a round at him. Suddenly he felt the sharp pain of a parabellum slug striking him in the side as he stumbled and fell to the floor.

The barbed pain in his ribs burned like fire, but still Minnevitch focused his entire concentration on the Nazi and on the certain death awaiting them if the detonator became fully armed.

Struggling to keep from blacking out, Minnevitch picked himself up from the floor and again lurched forward. He saw the Nazi colonel snarl as he raised the Walther, its muzzle aimed directly at his face.

And then time snapped back into synchronization again as Minnevitch lunged forward and his balled fist collided with Kreuger's jaw, smashing the cheekbone and dealing a lethal blow to the sensitive temple area.

The Walther in Kreuger's fist belched flame as it spat the deadly lead, but the shot was high and wild. Colonel Kreuger's hand released the handle of the detonator stirrup as he slid down the side of the bunker wall. The Walther fell from inert fingers, landing with a thud and a clatter.

As Kreuger hit the floor, broken and dead, Minnevitch hustled to one side and retracted the detonator lever back into the spring clamps that held it in a disarmed position, preventing the lethal circuit from being closed.

"Get the assault engineers here on the double!" the sergeant hollered at Mutt, then addressed the two Thunderbirds who ran into the room. "Amboy and Haystacks, stand guard over this switch. Anybody that's not in a khaki uniform gets it between the eyes, understood? How's Conners doing?"

"Dead, Sarge," Mutt said, not looking at anybody in particular as he stood over the badly charred corpse of the brave yet reckless GI. "Dead as you ever wanna get."

THE INTENSE FIGHTING to take the installation ended as quickly as it had begun. Outnumbered and suffering heavy casualties, the Germans soon lost their stomach for battle. Those among the Wehrmacht troops who had survived the onslaught wound up throwing down their guns and surrendering in large numbers.

A great cheer rose up from the victorious Thunderbirds and their British and Canadian allies as they herded the captured Nazis into sullen ranks and directed them to throw their arms in piles. The prisoners were herded into a hastily improvised holding area in a cordoned-off section of the wreckage-littered battle zone.

This arrangement would suffice until reinforcements from Sainte-Maxime could arrive. Along with the soldiers already deployed at the installation, the base could be held until the main Allied assault force reached the area the following day or the day after that.

The complete reversal of the fortunes of war had turned the tables on the Germans. Now it would be the goose-steppers who would be shipped to prisoner-of-war camps in America instead of Nazis marching Allied troops over the Rhine and into Nazi-controlled Berlin.

Whatever the final destiny of the captured German storm troopers, one thing was a certainty: as POWs, they would get a hell of a better shake at the hands of Uncle Sam than the American fighting man could have expected under the grim custody of the Nazis.

Watching the column of gray-cloaked storm troopers file into the holding area, Major Wynn Robnett waited for the Thunderbird radioman to tune captured Nazi equipment to the correct frequency for transmitting to American ground stations.

Having cooled his heels in the underground command bunker, now completely cleared of bodies and wreckage by the troops, the major was growing impatient as the corporal fiddled with the controls, producing loud squeals of interference. He had a message to get out, several messages, in fact. They were of the utmost importance and could not be delayed, no matter what the reason.

"Damn it, man, aren't you ready yet?" the major demanded from the radioman, a corporal from the 179th Infantry Regiment.

"Got it now, sir," the corporal finally said, then began speaking into the mike. "Red Dog Able to Reno One, stand by for a message from Major Robnett."

Robnett picked up the mike and began to speak. Suddenly he realized that he had a frog in his throat. The words came out of his mouth charged with raw emotion as he informed headquarters of the excellent news.

"At great sacrifice and loss of life and limb, elements of the 179th and 157th infantry regiments, along with British and Canadian forces, have secured the Nazi installation north-east of Alençon. We need weapons, medicine, food and reinforcements in a hurry."

"We read you, Major, over," said the voice of a ground-station radioman in a little while. "Please stand by."

It was Colonel Hackett who came on the line minutes later. Hackett congratulated Robnett and the battle-weary troops who had fought so bravely and without support to accomplish so much for so many.

"Paratroops are on the way. Supplies will be airlifted in, as well," Hackett informed Robnett. "Patch's Seventh Army is on the march and is expected to be in your area within forty-eight hours. Your instructions are to hold until relieved. Can you do it, Major?"

"We can sure as hell try, sir," he replied without a moment's hesitation.

"That's all anyone can expect of you." Then Hackett added, "Your troops have already earned the respect and the admiration of all of us. We won't let you down. Hold your position, Major, and may God bless you."

"Thank you, Colonel," Robnett returned. "Over and out."

Robnett handed back the handset to the radioman and suddenly felt every bit of his forty-seven years. He had spent most of his life in the service of his country, yet this was surely his finest hour.

It was ironic, in a way. Here he was, not having seen decent chow in months, unshaven, smelling like hell, with the soles of his combat boots worn down so much from his long captivity that they had more holes in them than leather.

But the major was smiling nonetheless. Yes, this was indeed his finest hour as a professional soldier and as an American.

He was damned proud of his men and proud of the great victory that their guts, grit and bravery had accomplished here today against nigh-on impossible odds.

Robnett would see to it personally that every damned one of them received the citations and the promotions they deserved. And when he handed out the medals, he would make sure that Sergeant Joe Minnevitch was the first GI in line. If any man had made this miraculous victory possible, it had been him.

There was still one final matter to be addressed. "Can you pipe me through to the men over a public-address channel?" Major Robnett wearily asked the radioman, rubbing his hot, tired eyes.

"No problem, sir," the corporal answered. "The krauts had a broadcast truck equipped with loud-speakers, and it's a wonder, but it has somehow escaped the bombing. I've already got a patch-through hooked up."

"Thank you, Corporal," Robnett said. Taking the microphone from the radioman, he searched for the words that could in some small way do justice to the accomplishments of the brave men he commanded, and knew that he could never hope to find those words, not in a million years.

He would try, though. Damn but he would try.

# TAKE 'EM NOW

## FOLDING SUNGLASSES
## FROM GOLD EAGLE

Mean up your act with these tough, street-smart shades. Practical, too, because they fold 3 times into a handy, zip-up polyurethane pouch that fits neatly into your pocket. Rugged metal frame. Scratch-resistant acrylic lenses. Best of all, they can be yours for only $6.99.

**MAIL YOUR ORDER TODAY.**

Send your name, address, and zip code, along with a check or money order for just $6.99 + .75¢ for delivery (for a total of $7.74) payable to Gold Eagle Reader Service.
(New York residents please add applicable sales tax.)

Remove from pouch | unfold once

unfold twice | and they're ready to wear

GES-1AR

**GOLD EAGLE**

Gold Eagle Reader Service
3010 Walden Avenue
P.O. Box 1396
Buffalo, N.Y. 14240-1396

---

*Offer not available in Canada.*